"HELLO, THE BOAT!"

"HELLO

BY PHYLLIS CRAWFOR

HENRY HOLT AN

THE BOAT!"

CTURES BY EDWARD LANING

OMPANY, NEW YORK

TO

CONSTANCE ROURKE

CONTENTS

"HELLO, THE BOAT!"

Chapter 1

FATHER TAKES A VOTE

FEBRUARY 8, 1817, was a Saturday to be remembered in the Doak family. During breakfast they talked about Father and wondered when he would return to Pittsburgh.

"It may be another month," said Mother soberly. "Let's see—he left on the first of November. It never takes less than three weeks to float down to New Orleans, and longer if he hits a snag or meets up with river pirates. Most likely he spent a few days in New Orleans selling his cargo and the timbers of the flatboat. Then there's the long journey afoot through the wilderness. If he got past the Natchez Trace without sickness or robbery he may be in Kentucky by now. But that's still a far piece from home."

The three young Doaks sighed—Susan, the oldest, who was sixteen, though she did not act it when the boys pulled her brown curls; Steve, the big overgrown redhead; and David, the stocky ten-year-old, who still wore gingham blouses with ruffled collars and could not keep his sandy hair smoothly brushed.

And then Mother dropped her two-pronged table fork. "Laws!" she said. "That means a man's coming!"

"I'll wager it's Father," said Steve.

"What fiddle-faddle!" said Susan with a superior smile. "A silly superstition."

"I'd as lief believe in this one," Mother admitted.

She got up from the breakfast table and tied a yellow gingham apron about her waist to protect her long blue linsey-woolsey dress. Then she poured a kettleful of hot water into the dishpan.

"Silly or not," said Steve, licking his knife clean, "I mean to stay at home today."

"What!" said Mother. "No sliding on the hill? No playing down at the shipyards?"

"No, ma'am," said Steve.

"Me neither," said David.

So Mother put them both to work scrubbing the unpainted pine floors while Susan aired the beds and changed the linen.

"Whether it's your father or the landlord," Mother said, "the house may as well be clean."

In the middle of the morning they heard Brownie and Patch, the pointers, barking in the yard. A few moments later someone was stamping the sooty snow off his boots on the stoop.

The whole family flew to the door just as Father himself walked in.

"What did I tell you?" Steve shrieked.

There were squeals of joy and a babble of questions as they all tried to hug him at the same time. His coonskin cap fell off and his knapsack slid to the floor.

"Hold on!" he cried. "I'm not fit to be seen until I've gotten out of my greasy old homespuns and shaved off these whiskers. Have you got any hot water, Miss Biddy?"

"First tell us how you got home so quickly," she said.

"Well," he said, "when I came to Maysville I heard the

Ohio packet needed another oarsman. So I worked my passage up river and saved time and shoe leather."

While the young people finished their tasks, shouting back and forth to one another, Mother prepared the wooden tub in the kitchen for Father's bath.

"Have you still got the bowl that fits my head, Miss Biddy?" he asked. "My hair needs cutting."

Mother laughed as she reached for the bowl on the shelf. "I reckon all that hair kept your neck pretty warm," she said.

While she cut his dark red hair around the edge of the bowl, he amused her with stories of gay New Orleans and the free life of the boatmen.

By the time he had bathed, shaved, and dressed up in his best blue pantaloons and a ruffled shirt with a linen neckcloth, the midday dinner was on the table and the young people were clamoring at the closed door.

Everybody was in high spirits during the meal. When they had barely finished their roast beef and potatoes, Father pushed back his hickory chair and stood up as if he were going to make a speech.

"Fellow countrymen by the name of Doak," he said, "the time has come for serious matters."

Susan and the boys giggled and laid down their pewter spoons to listen.

"I've made twenty trips down river since we left the farm in Virginia," Father continued. "We've managed to pay for your schooling and save nearly three thousand dollars to boot. I always calculated to quit the river when we got that much money and go back to raising a crop. But land's too dear in these parts, and none too rich."

"We can stay in Pittsburgh and both go back to teaching, George," said Mother.

"Hold on, Miss Biddy. I've got more to say. Times are hard here, rents are dear, and war prices are still on though the war was over in 1815. And that's true everywhere in the East. One out of every seven in New York City is living on charity, because there isn't enough work to go around."

"Wages are going down too," Steve put in. "Some of the carpenters down at the shipyards say if wages go much lower, all the poor men will organize trade unions like the printers and shoemakers."

"Yes," said Father, nodding, "I've heard talk of trade unions and of restricting emigration to keep out the Europeans, but that's all Eastern talk."

"Out with it, George," said Mother, resting her elbows on the table. "What do you aim to do?"

"I aim to convince all of you that it's time to pluck up stakes and move West, where there's elbowroom," Father said with a grin.

Mother and Susan gasped, but the boys whooped.

"Jumping jingoes, what a racket!" said Father. "Wait till I've finished. I don't calculate on going away out to the backlands. Cincinnati is plenty far. Farm land's cheap, living costs a third less, and there's good schools if the boys don't heed the long walk to the city. And if I find I can't make a decent living on the farm I can get work there during the winters."

"I want to go," said David excitedly. "I want to fight Indians."

Father laughed. "There aren't any Indians around Cincinnati now, Bub. But there's lots of chores to be done on a farm."

"I can do as much as a grown man," said Steve, "and Susan's clever at milking."

"Good!" said Father. "Now let's vote on it. How many Doaks want to go to Ohio?"

Five hands flew up, including Father's.

"When do we start?" asked Steve, squirming with impatience.

Father reached for his long-tailed coat and took two steps toward the door. "With the first high water this spring," he said. "But if I don't stir my stumps we won't have a boat in time. I'm going to see old Peter Cochran, and I'll be back with news in a couple of hours."

That afternoon nobody else left the house, although a group of boys with homemade sleds whistled at the picket gate for Steve and David, and two young ladies called to invite Susan to a candy-pull.

The whole family washed the dishes. In their excitement they jostled one another's elbows, dropped spoons, tripped over the dogs and even over their own feet.

Finally Mother put her hands over her ears.

"You children make so much noise I can't think," she said. "Why don't you go in the front room while I finish in the kitchen?"

Steve borrowed David's old slate and began to draw pictures on it, while Susan and David watched. At last Steve brushed a lock of his red hair out of his eyes and held up a finished picture.

"What's that?" he asked.

"It's either the 'Aetna' or the 'Vesuvius,'" David guessed.

"It might be the 'Oliver Evans,'" ventured Susan.

"It's the 'Vesuvius.' Look, she's a side-wheeler and she has two funnels and a sail. Anybody would know she was a Fulton and Livingston steamboat."

"I wouldn't," said Susan.

"You would if you were a boy," Steve said. "Hand me the sponge, Dave. I'll rub this one out and draw you another."

The next picture was of a smaller boat with its big wheel at the stern. Between the two funnels was a pilot's house, but no mast.

"The 'Enterprise'!" Both Susan and David recognized the boat this time.

"Right!" said Steve. "The boat that Captain Shreve and Father ran through the British blockade at New Orleans."

"Now draw the 'Washington,' Steve," David suggested.

Steve shook his head. "Don't you remember, I had the measles the only time she ever came to Pittsburgh. All I know is she's flat-bottomed and has the engine on deck instead of in the hold, and there's a second deck above. She's the only steamboat with a high-pressure engine, and she only has to stop once a day for wood."

"Steve, don't you wish we'd go down river on the 'Oliver Evans'? She's ready to start when the ice melts and the waters rise." David's face shone.

"I guess it would cost too much," said Steve gloomily. "We'll more likely get one of those awful Kentucky boats with a shed in the middle."

Almost as he spoke, the dogs scurried to the front door and barked.

"It's Father! Mother, hurry!" Susan called out.

When Father came in he was smiling broadly. He tweaked the boys' noses, pulled one of Susan's curls, and gave his wife such a hug that it took her off her feet.

"It's all fixed!" he shouted, rubbing his hands. "We'll go down river in style next month."

"Is old Peter building a flatboat for us?" asked Mother.

"No, I said 'in style,' Miss Biddy."

"Are we going on a keelboat?" asked David hopefully.

"No, Bub. What would a flatboat man do on a keelboat? I'm no alligator-horse."

"On the monthly packet boat?" Susan suggested.

Father shook his head.

"Not on a steamboat?" Steve's voice was full of awe.

Father laughed heartily. "And blow up halfway down river?"

"They don't all blow up," Steve said, flushing. "Captain Shreve never did—except once."

"I was only hectoring you, Red. I trust Henry Shreve myself. Well, I see you'll never guess. We're going to be masters of a storeboat!"

"A storeboat!"

Mother looked shocked. "Mercy on us, George Doak! How much will it cost?"

"Quite a few, I reckon," said Father cheerfully.

"George Doak, you've been hankering after a storeboat for ten years."

Father slapped his thigh and laughed again. "Well, when I walked into old Peter's workshop, he was drawing pictures of an elegant flatboat with three rooms and a store."

Mother smiled at him. "Are you certain you didn't ask old Peter to draw those pictures?"

"Miss Biddy, you have a suspicious nature," said Father. "Peter was talking to a Cincinnati merchant by the name of Riddle, who's here to lay in stock for his dry goods store and a line of New Orleans barges. He also wants a storeboat stout enough for the Western trade. Peter's building it for him, because we have better hard timber here and labor is cheaper than in Cincinnati."

"And he'll hire you as storemaster?"

"In a manner of speaking. He'll buy the stock, we'll trade along the way, and he'll give us a decent percentage of the profits."

"George Doak," Mother scolded, "you said it would cost a great deal of money."

"So I did, Miss Biddy, but you didn't ask whose money. This way we can change most of our savings into a bank draft and keep it to pay for our land and the new house."

"Oh, George!" Mother breathed.

"How much crew do we need, Father?" asked Steve.

Father looked grave. "We ought to have three men, including myself. The fewer the better, for money reasons. We'll need our money."

Steve straightened up. "You can count on me, Father. I can handle a pole or an oar."

Susan laid her hand on her father's sleeve. "I'm very strong for a girl, Father. You could teach me to help."

Father looked at her affectionately. "You've grown up to be a fine considerate young lady, Susie. I'm certain you'll be a help. You too, Red."

He rubbed his chin thoughtfully. "We might be able to manage, at that," he said.

Chapter II

BUSY DAYS

D URING the days that followed, the little frame cottage in Pittsburgh buzzed with activity. Every stick of furniture and every garment had to be considered, and either given away to some less fortunate family, or mended and set aside for the journey.

Day by day it grew harder for the young people to leave home for the Lancastrian school every morning. Susan, who helped the schoolmaster with the younger pupils while she finished her last year's studies, found that she could not keep her mind on their spelling and copy books.

Steve and David too had difficulties at school. The schoolmaster caught Steve drawing the "Enterprise" on a blank page at the back of his composition book, and kept him in after school until he had written one hundred times: "Experience keeps a dear school, but fools will learn in no other."

Almost every day David misspelled a word and had to write it a hundred times, his stubby fingers aching. As Susan remarked, it did improve his penmanship, but that was small comfort.

Once they reached home, however, there were high times. Father and Mr. Riddle made new purchases for the store-boat every day. Soon there was no space in the sitting room to sit. There were bolts and bolts of gay calicoes, ginghams and chintzes, and barrels, crates and packing boxes that piled higher toward the ceiling as the days passed.

As he wrote down the prices and quantity of each article in a big ledger, Father would display his wares.

"Now, President Monroe," he might say to David, "here is a pair of red suspenders fit for a ball, and a bandanna handkerchief to match. But if you prefer them, I have some elegant English leghorn bonnets that might become you. And how is the White House fixed for red earthenware milkpans and stoneware churns? Would you like to see some of our best scythes, axes, Barlow knives, woven stockings, saddles, whitewood bowls and spoons, combs, pocket compasses, tinware for the kitchen, Pittsburgh green glass, or perhaps some of Page and Bakewell's clear flint glass? Don't be a ninnyhammer, Mr. President. Step right up and buy anything you want."

Then Mother would interrupt. "George, George, you're a ninnyhammer yourself, keeping the children from their chores. The cow has to be milked and the butter churned. Besides, here it is nearly March. Susan has mending to do, and the boys promised to polish the pewter with wood ashes."

"Well, they have to learn the stock," Father said. "The best way to learn anything is by playing games."

"I wish you'd say that to the schoolmaster," Steve chuckled.

"He wouldn't believe me," said Father. "But we'll try it on the boat. Do you hear that, Miss Biddy? No schoolroom on the boat."

Mother looked a little dubious. "The children will lose

out in their studies. I'd feel easier in my mind if I heard their lessons every day."

"Well, you might have spelling bees, Miss Biddy, and lessons out of Morse's *Geography Made Easy*," Father conceded. "But no arithmetic. Susan will keep the account books, and the boys can learn their arithmetic by helping her and making change."

One cold Saturday afternoon Father bundled up the whole family in their blue and green woolen caps and mittens and marched them down to the waterfront along the Monongahela. Their feet crunched the frozen ground and the wind whistled past their ears.

"We're not going to see our storeboat," said Father as they walked along. "We're going to learn about broadhorns."

They arrived at the water's edge. All up and down the river, barges and rafts were held fast by the ice near the shore. Near the Fulton shipyard lay the steamboat "Oliver Evans," waiting for spring.

At the landing place of the Ohio packet boats, nine men were hacking away at the ice with axes. While they chopped, the monthly packet and a slim keelboat waited in the open river. The blue-coated keelboatmen leaned on their long poles to keep their boat from drifting.

"Hello, the boats!" Father roared.

An answering shout came from the packet. "Hello, Doak!"

One of the keelboatmen waved his coonskin cap and sang out, "Hello, the smoke-covered soot-eaters! Why don't you stop burning pit-coal in your town? How can you tell when the sun's shining?"

Father waved good-naturedly. "How's the ice down river, you alligator-horses?" he yelled.

The cold wind blew the answer back from the keelboat. "Frozen nineteen inches deep at Marietta. Couldn't even land."

Father shook his head. "All this cold weather looks bad for an early start," he said.

David swung his arms and jigged to get warm. "Father," he said, "is that the packet you came home on?"

"No, it's another one. But I reckon that one will carry Mr. Riddle back to Cincinnati next week. Well, here's a broadhorn."

He pointed out a low, covered boat with a flat roof, moored to several stakes in the hard ground.

"But where are the oars that make the boat look like a broadhorn steer?" asked Susan.

"The sweeps? Oh, they're put up for the winter," explained Father. "But you can see the pivots they rest on, there on the roof toward the bows. Down below on the deck there's another pivot for the gouger, the small oar used for steering when the current is very bold. Now, can you boys tell me which is the most important oar of all?"

"That's simple," said Steve. "The steering oar."

"Where is it?"

"Well, it rests on that pivot at the back of the roof," said Steve, pointing with his mittened hand.

"Why is it at the stern and on the roof?" asked Father.

"Well," said Steve carefully, "I guess it's easier to steer at the back of a boat, and you have to be as high up as possible, so you can see where you're going."

"Right!" said Father. "Now we're going home and practice navigation."

"What?" Mother asked. She blew into her blue mittens to warm her hands.

"Wait and see."

They did practice navigation that afternoon. Father moved Steve's bed into the middle of the boys' room, and directed Mother to sit cross-legged at the head.

He handed her a fire shovel and asked, "What's this?"

"It looks like a shovel to me," she said.

"Oh, no, Mother," Steve said, his blue eyes sparkling. "I'll wager it's the gouger, because you're at the bows of the boat. Isn't that right, Father?"

"Right. Now, Steve, you take the hardest post. You sit at the foot with this mop. What's its name?"

David began to jump up and down. "I know, I know. It's the steering oar."

"That's right. Susan and Dave, you get two brooms and man the sweeps. Are you ready?"

"Yes!"

"You're about to leave a landing place on the Kentucky shore. You want to get out into the channel. Miss Biddy, what do you do?"

"I turn my gouger to the right," said Mother, giving a twist to the fire shovel.

"Wrong," said Father sternly. "The current isn't swift near the shore. We don't need the gouger."

"Then I push off from shore with my sweep, don't I, Father?" Susan asked.

"Impossible," said Father.

David began to bounce on the bed. "I know!"

"Watch out! You're rocking the boat," Father cautioned him.

David giggled and sat back. "But I know. I'm the one that pushes off, ain't I?"

"Why?"

"Because Kentucky is on the left bank. Susan hasn't any land to push against."

"That's right," said Father, smiling. "Now what are you doing, Steve?"

"I'm heading her out toward the current, like this, and then I straighten my oar and let her drift."

"That's the most important thing of all," said Father, "to let her drift with the current. You don't have to steer hard except when you want to go around some obstacle in your path."

They tried it again, then shoved off from the Ohio side for a change. They made a landing, first on one side of the river and then on the other. Then Father made them take the bed down a riffle, where Mother had to use her fire shovel.

Attracted by the shouts of laughter, Patch and Brownie finally left their comfortable quarters behind the kitchen stove, and barked and leaped at the sweeps with such enthusiasm that the lesson had to be brought to a close.

With a whoop Steve dived off the bed and swam out of the room on all fours.

"That reminds me," said Mother. "It's Saturday and time for everybody to have a swim in the tub down in the kitchen."

Chapter III

THE STOREBOAT

DESPITE an alarming cold snap which lasted from the middle of February through the first week in March, spring came early and suddenly. Two days of warm drizzling rain in the middle of March loosened the ice and thawed the ground. The frozen streets became mud overnight, and up and down the river one could hear the cracking of the ice as it broke away from the shore and floated down the river.

All along the riverfront one heard the shouts of workmen and the ringing of hammers. Old boats were being calked and repainted, and new boats were taking shape under the tools of the ship carpenters.

Swelled by melting snow and ice and by the rains, the Monongahela and the Allegheny were rising steadily. The Ohio river, which begins at their junction at Pittsburgh, was in fine order for all descending craft.

One Thursday a man went through the city tacking up posters which announced that the name of the "Oliver Evans" had been changed to the "Constitution," and that she would start on her maiden voyage down the river on the following day. At noon on Friday the new steamboat gave a shrill whistle and chugged away from the Fulton and Livingston landing on the Monongahela. Father, standing on the bank when she left, could hear her clanking engine long after she had disappeared around the bend.

At last on Monday the twenty-fourth of March, 1817, the storeboat was ready. As soon as Father brought the news, Mother put on her bonnet and cloak and they went to the schoolhouse to fetch Susan and the boys.

The whole schoolroom burst into an uproar when the Doaks gathered up their textbooks and made their farewells. Noisy good-bys followed them out into the street, although the schoolmaster shouted for silence and rapped on his desk with a ruler.

Too excited to speak, the family tramped westward along the plank sidewalks. When they arrived at the banks of the muddy Monongahela, the storeboat lay before them, rocking gently with the current. She was a big broadhorn painted slate blue. The six small casement windows, three on each side, were trimmed with bright red. A red canoe rested on the deck against the rear wall of the cabin, beside the ladder. At the forward end of the boat was a fenced enclosure for the livestock.

Susan gasped. "Why, she's bigger than any boat on the river! She looks like Noah's ark."

"Oh, there are bigger boats," said Father. "Steamboats, seagoing vessels, even broadhorns. I've seen plenty of New Orleans boats a hundred feet long. Last year below Cincinnati I saw a blacksmith's boat big enough to hold a complete forge, a wagon and a team of horses."

"The roof seems mighty low," said Mother. "George, are you sure you can stand upright inside the boat?"

The boys laughed. "I guess you don't know much about

boats, Mother," said Steve. "The floors of the cabins are lower than the deck. They're below the water level."

"How do we get in?" asked Susan.

"Well," said Father, "you could take an ax and chop your way in, but I prefer the main hatch. That's the sliding trap door in the roof down near the stern. There's also a little door from the kitchen into the pen for the livestock, but there's no ladder there."

"Let's go on board," Mother suggested.

Father leaped to the deck, vaulted to the low roof, and tugged at one of the sweeps. The storeboat swung closer to the shore.

"Tighten the moorings there, Steve," he called down.

Steve drew up the slack in the rope by which the boat was tied to shore, and made another knot. Now the storeboat was near enough for even David's short legs to make the jump.

The boat smelled of new clean pine wood. Climbing down the hatchway, they found themselves in the store. It was a big room with windows on two sides, and shelves lining the walls from floor to ceiling. There were two long counters, one on each side of the room, and a stepladder for reaching the top shelves.

Father stepped behind one of the counters and laid his palms flat on the bare surface.

"What can I show you?" he said solemnly.

Susan pointed to the empty shelves behind him. "I'll take twenty of those lanterns."

"Only twenty?" said Father. "Why, madam, you ought to carry at least fifty if you expect to travel far after nightfall."

"Come, come, George," said Mother. "No dillydallying. We must make haste if we want to move into the boat tomorrow."

"All right, Miss Biddy. Follow me."

He led them down the narrow hall and threw open a door on the left.

"Here is where the young Doaks sleep," he said. "Across the hall is the old Doaks' cabin. Straight ahead is the kitchen."

They peered into the little rooms and then walked into the big kitchen. An iron cooking stove was already set up in the center of the room with its pipe running up through the ceiling. There were two windows on opposite walls. In a corner facing the doorway, three steps led up to the little door which opened into the pen at the bows. Most of the wall space was taken up by cabinets and shelves. There was even a row of pothooks waiting for the cooking pots.

Mother looked about with a practiced eye. "I guess we'll be very comfortable here, George."

"Mr. Riddle built her for a family boat," Father explained. "He has some notion of trying to send her up the Wabash this fall. But I'm afraid he'll need a mighty big crew to take her upstream, whether he has her rowed or towed."

The boys and Susan left Mother and Father in the kitchen while they made one more complete tour of the storeboat. Then Mother herded them all home to finish their preparations for the journey.

The next day Father hired a team and wagon and two helpers. With a great deal of puffing and shouting the men gradually cleared the sitting room of barrels and crates and stacked them high in the wagon.

Meanwhile Mother and Susan were packing the trunks and portmanteaus. David was in demand to sit on the lids while Steve tugged at the ropes to bind them.

Now and then a neighbor ran in to say good-by and to leave a cake, a loaf of fresh bread, or a pie as a parting gift. One old friend brought a steaming beef roast. From time to time young people who had grown up with Susan and the boys dropped in and stood around for a while, but no one had time for conversation.

The wagon drove off with the first load. An hour or more later, Father and the two men returned and began to move out the furniture. Chests of drawers, chairs, a big table, trunks, boxes of household goods, and unwieldy rolls of blankets, quilts and featherbeds, all were piled into the wagon. The Eli Terry clock was taken down from the wall, still ticking, and propped up against the inside of the wagon. The house was left bare.

Last of all, on the back of the wagon they tied the coop containing the three geese, and a larger coop of speckled chickens.

"Now," said Father, wiping the perspiration from his forehead, "Miss Biddy, you and Susan hop up beside the driver. I'll walk behind to see that nothing falls off. Boys, you can follow with Bessie and the dogs."

The driver cracked his whip and the wagon rattled off down the street. The astonished fowls in their coops set up a cackling and honking that could be heard for blocks.

Steve and David looked at each other. The last of their friends had said good-by and left. Without a word they turned and walked through the house, with Brownie and Patch brushing against their linsey-woolsey pantaloons. Their footsteps echoed in the empty rooms.

Steve kept his eyes straight before him. "Don't look, Dave," he said. "It'll make you feel funny."

David nodded and blinked. As they went through the kitchen, he noticed a bone that one of the dogs had left under the old stove. He picked it up and thrust it into his pocket. Steve did not see him.

Once out in the street, leading the red Devonshire cow by a rope halter, Steve began to whistle. David broke into a hop and a skip, and the dogs frisked along beside him.

"I guess this is the last time we'll ever go down this street, ain't it, Steve?"

"I'd just as lief never see it again," said Steve, with a show of cheerfulness.

"Me too." David put his hands in his pockets, found the old bone and tossed it away. It clattered against a fence post.

"What was that?" asked Steve.

David reddened. "Nothing."

It was easy enough to lead Bessie to the storeboat, but it took five men half an hour to hoist her on board, and then she skidded and mooed uneasily with every gentle motion of the boat.

"She'll be all right when the load of hay comes," said Father. "Have the men pile the hay in one corner of her shed, Steve, and scatter a little hay all over the pen. Meanwhile you can put some water in her trough."

"Shall I turn the chickens and geese loose, Father?"

"Not until you clip one wing to keep them from flying off the boat. Dave can help you."

By the time the boys had finished their work in the pen, the wagon was unloaded and the two helpers had driven away. Steve had to stoop to go through the little doorway into the kitchen, but it was high enough for David.

Mother's head appeared over a pile of boxes in the middle of the kitchen floor.

"Come, boys," she said. "Father wants help. He's putting the stock on the shelves in the store."

They climbed over the boxes and followed her through the narrow hall. Although it was chilly inside, Father had his sleeves rolled up and his rough brown shirt unfastened at the neck.

"Let's start with the shelves on our right," he was saying. "That can be the leather department. Here, Steve, find the stepladder and start piling the saddles on the top shelves. Dave, the shoes are in that crate at the foot of the hatchway ladder. They can go on the lower shelves."

"I'd like to fix the cloth goods," Susan proposed. "Where do you want them, Father?"

"Next section," said Father. "Beyond the window, ready-made pantaloons, jackets, hats and bonnets. On the other wall, Yankee notions such as needles, pins, thread, ribbons, artificial flowers, jewelry and gimcracks. Over behind the ladder, tea and spices, pots and pans, then crockery, glass, woodenware, pewter and brass. Over by the other window, hardware for farmers. The scythes can be stacked in the corner. Then hardware for builders—nails, hinges, latches and such."

"What goes on the shelves at the left of the hall?" asked Mother.

"That's the book store," Father replied.

"Books?" Heads popped up from behind the counter, from packing boxes and barrels. "Books?"

"Books," said Father.

"But you didn't show them to us," wailed Susan.

"I didn't show you the nails either," said Father.

"How many books did Mr. Riddle choose, George?"

"Oh, enough to keep the Doak family busy. A fine lot of Bibles, catechisms, almanacs, Webster's *Unabridged Dictionary*."

David's face fell. "Is that all?"

"Well, I reckon there are a few more. There's *Robinson Crusoe, Pilgrim's Progress, The Vicar of Wakefield*, the works of Shakespeare, Washington Irving's *History of New York* by Diedrich Knickerbocker, *Gulliver's Travels*, Scott's *Waverley, Tom Jones*, the six volumes of Franklin's works. But maybe you'd rather read some of our elegant primers and spellers, Bub."

David made a dive for his father.

"Run, Father! Dave's going to give you a licking!"

"Here, here," said Mother. "Don't wreck Mr. Riddle's boat until after we've fixed it up."

For a while they worked quietly, sorting, carrying and arranging on shelves. Finally Steve unearthed a pair of scales.

"Where does this belong?" he asked. "In the notions?"

"That's not for sale," said Father. "It stays on the counter near the hardware store, to weigh nails."

"Can't we get rid of some of these empty crates and barrels?" Mother asked.

"Yes," said Father. "Steve, you and Dave carry them into the kitchen, if there's any room in there. We'll chop them up for stove wood."

"Wait," said Mother, "three of those barrels ought to be put up on the roof to catch the rain against wash day."

"River water's all right for washing, Miss Biddy."

"I don't like the look of it, George. Besides, rain water is softer."

"All right, boys," said Father. "Carry three barrels to the roof."

At last the store was ready. The shelves were piled high to overflowing, the counters were scrubbed and the floor was swept. The aroma of fresh clean fabrics, spices, and well-cured leather mingled with the resinous smell of the pine.

Father climbed the steep stairs to the roof and came back down, scanning the shelves as though he had never seen them before.

"It looks elegant," he said, rubbing his hands. "The first thing you see is the cloth, all the colors of the rainbow. Altogether it looks like a fine chance of wares. But I've forgotten something. Hand me a yardstick, a hammer and seven little nails, Dave."

On the edge of the counter nearest the dry goods he measured off a yard and its fractions, and drove in nails as markers.

"We'll have those markers worn out in no time," he said. "Now we must tie a good sharp pair of scissors to the counter to cut the goods. If we don't nail the scissors down,

we'll either sell them by mistake or use them to cut firewood."

"I wish we had a fire," Susan said, hugging herself to keep
warm. "I'm cold as soon as I stand still."

"And I'm hungry," David complained.

"Laws!" Mother exclaimed. "I forgot all about dinner!
I'm glad the neighbors supplied us with enough to eat."

After a long search among the boxes in the kitchen, she
located the roast beef, bread and a knife. They ate a cold
dinner perched on packing cases, and threw tidbits of meat
to Brownie and Patch, who suddenly appeared from behind
a chest of drawers.

When they had finished eating, everybody helped set the
living quarters to rights. All the pots were unpacked and
hung on their hooks along the kitchen wall. The dishes and
tableware were piled up on the shelves. Father drove a nail
in the wall beside the doorway and hung up the wooden
clock, which still kept good time but no longer struck the
hours.

Steve got the ax and began to reduce the packing boxes
to a neat stack of firewood beside the stove.

"Take care that you don't chop the floor instead of the
wood, Red," Father warned.

The kitchen now began to look like a real room. Under
one window was the long dinner table, with three hickory
chairs on each side. Under the opposite window was another table, which held three big brown stoneware crocks
for drinking water, the dishpan, the wash basin, and a bar
of yellow soap. Father hung a mirror beside the window,
above the end of the table, and drove several nails into the
wall for towels.

He stepped back and looked at himself in the mirror. "That's a good light for shaving," he said. "And better for face washing. A little high for Davie, but fine for the rest of us."

Next the bedrooms were put in order. The featherbeds were unrolled and laid on the floor for mattresses. Then came two smooth blue calico sheets for each bed, and a light featherbed on top for warmth.

In each bedroom was a chest of drawers. Mother and Susan unpacked the clothes from the portmanteaus and one of the trunks, and laid them away neatly in the drawers. Father stacked all the other trunks in one corner of his and Mother's room, where there was plenty of space.

"Now," said Mother, shutting the last drawer, "I guess that's all for today, except supper and the milking."

Father dusted off his hands. "No, there's one thing more. We haven't a flag."

He went into the store and snipped off a large square of yellow calico.

"There," he said, handing the calico to Susan. "You can hem it to keep it from fraying, while Steve and I put up a flagstaff at the bows."

Susan turned the piece over in her hands. "But, Father," she said, "wouldn't a red flag look better? It would match the trimming on the windows, and the canoe."

"Red would look better," Father admitted. "But only grocery boats fly a red flag. Yellow means dry goods, and that's us."

Chapter IV

THE FIRST VISITOR

BY sundown everything on the storeboat was in order. Bessie had been milked, and the pailful of warm frothy milk had been poured into a shallow milk-pan to let the cream rise. The chickens and geese had hopped up on their low roosts and settled down for the night with contented murmurings and cluckings.

In the kitchen a fire roared in the iron cooking stove. The two dogs lay stretched out on the floor in front of the stove, so that Mother had to step over them to reach the potatoes and eggs sizzling in the frying pans.

"How about hands and faces?" asked Mother, as she took the warm plates out of the oven. "Is everybody washed? Davie, let Susan see your ears and neck."

"He must be clean, Mother," Susan said. "See how dirty his towel is."

"My towel's no worse than Steve's," David protested.

"That ain't mine," said Steve with a grin. "It's Father's."

"Come, come," said Father. "We're wasting time. Can't you see supper is ready?"

When they were all seated at the table, Mother said, "This is the first real meal in a new home. George, will you ask the blessing?"

Father bowed his head, and for a moment, there was no sound except the ticking of the old Connecticut clock.

"Bless this food to our use and us to Thy loving service, O Lord. Amen."

"Amen," the others murmured.

Father looked around the table and smiled. "I reckon this is going to be my most profitable trip down river."

"Are we going to make lots of money?" David asked.

"I wasn't thinking of money, Bub. I was thinking how lucky I am to have you all with me. I'd like to propose a toast to the happy future."

Everyone raised his cup of milk. "To the happy future!"

"Now to James Monroe, our new president. May his tour of the West bring him a broader understanding of his office."

"And may his coach keep right side up in the mud holes," Mother added feelingly.

When the room began to get dark, Mother lighted a candle and set it on the table. Father threw another chunk into the fire.

"Let's sing 'Hail Columbia,'" David suggested. "I know all the words now."

They all sang, with more vigor than melody. As the last note died down, they heard a shout from the shore.

"Hello, the boat!"

Steve ran to the window and threw it open. "It's a man with a lantern. Hello, the lantern!"

"I heard the singing," the voice boomed again. "May a stranger come aboard and join in the merrymaking?"

Father stepped to the window. "Welcome, stranger. I'll come out on deck to show you the way."

He lighted another candle at the flame of the first one and carried it with him. The others heard him climb the little ladder to the roof. In a few minutes the sound of voices mingled with the heavy tread of the two men. When they appeared in the kitchen doorway, Father was smiling.

"This," he said, "is General William Henry Harrison, who knows every man, woman and child in the West and is sure to be president one day."

The general, a big ruddy man with a prominent nose, swept off his white beaver hat and bowed low.

"Your servant," he said.

Mother rose and gave him her hand. "This is an unexpected pleasure," she said.

Susan pushed back her chair and curtsied politely, while the boys stepped up to shake hands.

Father took the tall white hat and helped the general remove his long-tailed green broadcloth overcoat.

David, his brown eyes wide with astonishment, stared at the visitor's fine white linen stock and frilled shirt front, the elegant tailed coat of green serge, the cream-colored breeches and polished black shoes.

"Sir," he blurted out, "surely you're not the same General Harrison who was an Indian fighter."

The general chuckled as he spread the tails of his coat and sat down. "The same," he said.

"But did you fight in those clothes?" David persisted.

The others smiled.

"Hardly, my boy," the general rumbled. "But I've got to dress like a member of Congress now. Have you never heard the old saying, 'When at Rome, do as the Romans do'?"

He looked across the table at Mother. "When I hallooed from the bank," he said, "I had no idea the boat belonged to my good friend, Riddle, or that I'd find George Doak in charge. And certainly I didn't dream I'd have the pleasure of meeting two such handsome young women as yourself and your daughter, madam."

"I'm afraid you're a flatterer, General," said Mother.

"Not at all, madam. A man in my position must always tell the truth."

Steve hitched his chair nearer. Patch wriggled up and laid her spotted head on his knee.

"I've heard about your bravery during the war with England, sir," he said. "Ain't you the one they call the 'Washington of the West'?"

"My countrymen paid me that honor," the general said. He patted Steve's red head. "A fine big boy, Doak. Are you going to join the militia in another year or two, my boy?"

"No, sir. I hope it won't be necessary."

"What!" The general drew back in surprise. "After I've introduced my bill in the Congress?"

"Which one is that?" asked Father. "The militia bill?"

"Yes, proposing compulsory military training in all the schools of America. Every citizen a soldier. I tell you, Doak, we need armed forces to push our way into the prairies. Young man, why don't you want to be a soldier?"

Steve flushed, but his blue eyes were steady. "I'm not a coward, sir, and I'm a prime hunter. But I thought the wars were all over."

The general shook with laughter. "I advise you to study the history of Rome and Sparta, my boy. You'll learn what happens to a nation weakened by peace and luxuries."

David spoke up. "I'm going to be a soldier, sir. I'm

going to be an Indian fighter, and then when I've killed all the Indians, I'm going to be a keelboatman."

"There speaks a fierce lad after my own heart," the general said heartily. "I don't think we need to kill all the Indians, but we do need to show our strength. By the way, lad, the musket and the boatman's pole are not an impossible combination. I'm a good pilot myself."

"How are you going down river?" asked Father.

"My good friend Gorham Worth has engaged me as pilot for his flatboat. We leave Pittsburgh tomorrow."

"So do we," said Father.

"Good! We shall meet again." He turned to Steve. "My boy, you remind me of my son William. He doesn't care for the army either. He wants to put his money into steamboats."

"Steamboats!" Steve sat up.

"Yes, he has a notion he can control the mail line and run the packets out of business. But I'm afraid he'll be disappointed."

"Our Steve wouldn't agree with you, General," said Father. "And I'm not sure I would. Henry Shreve convinced me in the Battle of New Orleans."

"Well, I admit that steamboats were useful on the lower Mississippi in the late war. But they will never conquer the Ohio."

Steve shook his head vigorously. "But, sir—"

Mother gave him a warning glance. "Be careful of contradicting, son."

"Mother," said Susan, "look at Davie."

The little boy had slumped down in his chair and his

fair head had begun to nod. Father leaned over and shook him gently.

"It's time you were in bed, Bub."

David staggered to his feet, mumbled a sleepy good night, and stumbled into the little bedroom.

Father tossed another chunk of wood into the fire, and the talk went on.

"It's my firm belief," said the general, "that we don't need steamboats on the Ohio. When the National Road is extended from Wheeling through the West, we won't have to depend upon the river."

"But I thought both Madison and Monroe were against the National Road," said Father.

"They are. But it's only a question of funds. They say it's a violation of state rights to appropriate federal money to improvements within any state boundary."

"Do you think the Congress will vote the money to finish the road anyway?"

"I'm confident of it," said the general. "Anything of such importance to the entire West is bound to be constitutional. Mark my words, Doak. We'll have the National Road extended, and we'll have a canal connecting Lake Erie with the Hudson river."

Then the conversation veered to the subject of slavery.

"I hear a heap of talk against slavery," Father said. "In the hills of Virginia where I come from, there were mighty few slave-owners and I guess they were pretty good masters. But I'd rather have my boys grow up in a free state."

The general nodded slowly. "I'm a Virginian by birth too," he said, "but I firmly believe that the commercial future of this country lies in the free states."

As the talk took this sober turn, Susan and Steve began to yawn. Before long they stole away to bed. Too tired to heed the rocking of the boat, they fell asleep almost as soon as their heads touched the pillows.

Chapter V

DOWN THE RIVER

THE next morning they were wakened by the crowing of cocks up and down the river. Their own cock flapped his wings and tried to outcrow a rival on a near-by raft which housed a family of eight New Englanders, two tabby cats, a horse, three cows, five hogs, and a large number of chickens.

After a hurried breakfast, the Doaks flew to their chores. By the time the sun had begun to shine weakly through the haze of smoke over Pittsburgh, the dishes were washed, red Bessie was milked, and the featherbeds had been shaken out of the window. The bills of the fowls drummed on the deck as they pecked at their corn.

"All hands on deck!" Father cried. "Here we go. David, cast off the fasts. That's right. Now jump on board before she swings out from shore. Steve, take the right sweep, Susie the left. I'll man the steering oar."

"What shall I do?" asked Mother.

"You're the passenger, Miss Biddy. Ready? Set off, Steve."

Steve puffed and strained as he pushed his long sweep against the bank.

"Easy there!" Father warned. "We barely missed that raft."

The storeboat creaked and groaned her way out into the

channel of the Monongahela. Once in the current, she moved smoothly down the muddy river. Patch and Brownie pattered up and down the deck, now rushing forward to bark at Bessie through the bars, now running back to leap at the roof where Father stood.

Men looked up from their work along the banks and shouted. Small boys flourished their woolen caps. Housewives leaned over their back fences and waved their calico aprons. And the yellow flag at the bows fluttered in the morning breeze.

As they swung past a low Kentucky boat, partly roofed over, General Harrison appeared in the doorway of the cabin and waved. He wore coarse brown pantaloons, a rough shirt open at the throat, and a coonskin cap like Father's.

"Yesterday a Congressman, today a boatman," he called out genially. "I'll overtake you later."

The storeboat rounded the point of old Fort Du Quesne and steered between the Monongahela bar and the Allegheny bar formed by the silt carried down from the hills.

"Put up your sweeps!" Father shouted. "Steve, fetch the horn and blow a good long blast."

Steve got the big red tin horn and blew until he was dizzy.

"That's to scare off the devil and secure good luck," Father explained. "We're on the Ohio river now."

They could still trace the clear swift waters of the Allegheny in the wide Ohio even an hour or two later, when they began to pass the first of the river's many willow-covered islands.

"We have to keep to the right here," said Father, "or McKee's Rocks will stave us in."

Now that they were out of the murky atmosphere of Pittsburgh, the sun shone clear and the air was soft and full of damp earthy smells. Father and the boys soon peeled off their blue jerkins, but Susan in her short-sleeved green linsey-woolsey found her little plaid spencer none too warm until she moved over beside the hot smoking chimney.

She could hear Mother rattling pans below, but she could not tear herself away from the river. The waters were so high that they lapped the roots of the bare trees along the banks. There were occasional clearings between forests of oak, walnut, sugar maple, and beech, and sometimes a wisp of blue smoke rose from a cabin hidden in the woods.

"When are we going to stop and sell things, Father?" David asked, swinging his feet over the edge of the roof.

"Jumping jingoes!" Father exclaimed. "I'm glad you reminded me. I forgot all about the store."

Susan laughed. "Did you think you were going all the way to New Orleans again?"

"I reckon I did, at that. Well, I doubt that we'd sell very much so close to Pittsburgh. Do you mark that old fellow in yonder field? I'll wager he's planting his peas and radishes. It's about time."

"Ask him, Father," Steve suggested.

"Hello, the peas and radishes!" Father yelled.

The answer came back across the water. "Hello, the boat! Have you got any indigo aboard the boat?"

"Plenty! Stand to your sweeps, children. Davie, blow the horn."

The sound of the horn echoed against the wooded hills. Father cast an eye upstream to see if any craft were approaching and then steered for the bank. The big boat shuddered as the current struck her side, but Father braced himself and held her until she nosed into the soft bank a little farther downstream.

"Jump ashore, Dave, and wind the rope around that poplar tree. Keep her steady with the sweeps, children. After this we'll blow that horn every time we see any signs of life."

The whiskered farmer emerged from the leafless underbrush at the edge of the field.

"You must know something about farms, stranger," he said, "or you wouldn't have known what I was a-planting."

Father chuckled. "I was raised on a farm."

"Then I guess you know how tetchy a woman gets when she runs out of something between market days. My old woman used up all her bluing last Monday, and she's been pestering me to leave my planting and go to the city for some more. I'm right glad to see you."

Father reached out a hand to help him jump on board.

The farmer turned and looked back. "Tarnation!" he exclaimed. "Ain't that like the old woman? I guess she's coming to help me pick out that indigo."

Across the sunny field from the weather-beaten farmhouse trudged a tall well-built woman in a red calico dress and brown shawl, followed by a long line of children of all ages, barefoot in spite of the chilly air.

"Suffering rattlesnakes and pumpkins!" Father burst out. "Are they all yours, stranger?"

"I guess so," replied the farmer. "They all call me Paw and I ain't picked up no strays."

The "old woman" and all the young ones swarmed over the edge of the deck, climbed to the roof and followed

Father down the hatchway into the store. Susan took her place at the money box, and wrote the date, March 26, 1817, at the top of the first page of the account book.

Father, with a pencil behind his ear, pulled out Barlow knives, pocket compasses, combs, ribbons and other things.

"We have lots more than indigo aboard," he said.

"Well," said the farmer, "last week there was two store-boats blew their horns and stopped, but I had neither money nor goods to swap. You come at a good time, storemaster. I sold a two-year-old working horse yesterday for fifty dollars."

His flock of towheaded children began to whisper among themselves, and to point at various articles on the shelves.

"How much can we spend?" his wife asked, tucking the ends of her brown shawl into her belt.

"Oh, I guess we can spare about one gold eagle."

"Ten whole dollars!" The murmur went around the room and rose to a shout as the barefoot children crowded around their father.

"Pappy, buy me a Barlow knife!"

"Pappy, can I have a book?"

"Pappy! Pappy!"

"Pick out any gimcracks you want," said the farmer, smiling through his whiskers.

His wife raised her clear voice. "Be quiet, children. If there's an eagle to spend, your mammy will spend it. There's too much we need, to waste money on gimcracks and nick-nacks."

"There's a woman of spirit!" cried Mother Doak from the doorway. "I'll help you."

The children watched quietly while the two women chose

iron and tin pots, spices and essences, white queen's ware crockery, and a paper of indigo. The farmer's wife had Father measure off yards of yellow, green, red and blue gingham for spring dresses and jackets. Then with a smile she selected copies of *Robinson Crusoe*, *Gulliver's Travels* and *The Vicar of Wakefield*.

Susan made a list of the purchases and added up the prices. "It comes to ten dollars and forty-two cents," she announced.

"That's too much," said Mother Doak firmly. "We'll subtract the forty-two cents."

"Miss Biddy," said Father, "have you forgotten that we're selling, not buying? We ought to add on more."

"I think the lady is right," said the farmer. "I never argue with a lady."

The little gold coin jingled into the money box, and the small army seized their spoils and marched off the boat. They lined up on the bank to wave while the storeboat cast off and swung back into the middle of the river.

The young Doaks sat down again on the roof.

"That was fun," David said. "Let's sell some more."

"I hope we'll do as well every time we stop," Father remarked.

Suddenly Steve pointed up the river. "There comes a Kentucky boat fastened to a raft. They're going to bump us if you don't look out, Father."

Father leaned hard on the steering oar and the storeboat swerved to the right.

"Hello, the boat!" came a familiar booming voice.

"It's the general!" Steve shouted.

General Harrison stepped to the edge of the Kentucky boat and called, "Doak, keep alongside, will you? I want to buy a couple of pounds of tea for my friends on the raft. It may be years before they see any luxuries again."

Two little boys on the raft behind smiled and held up a large cheese and a loaf of baker's bread, and pointed to the general.

"Susan," said Father, "make haste and get the tea for the general before he gives away all his provisions. He's up to his old tricks."

She scurried down the ladder and grabbed two packages of China tea. Without stopping to note the sale in the account book, she ran back up to the roof and tossed the packages to General Harrison.

"Well done, lass," he boomed, as he caught them. "You have a pretty aim as well as a pretty face."

Something whirled through the air and fell at her feet. When she stooped to pick it up, she found that it was a mesh purse containing four silver dollars.

"This is far too much, sir," she said, and raised her arm to throw the purse back to him.

The general waved the matter aside. "Keep the rest," he said. "Buy a ribbon for your curls, and a top for each of the boys. Good-by! Good-by, Doak, and good luck!"

The two lighter craft glided past the storeboat and continued down the river.

Susan stood there with the purse in her hands. "What shall I do with this money, Father?"

"I want a red top," said David.

"Let's forget about ribbons and tops," said Father, keeping his eyes on the river. "It goes into the money box as payment for two pounds of tea."

"I don't want a top anyway," said Steve. "I'd much

rather spend the money for powder and lead shot. I mean to go hunting when we get to Ohio."

"Susan," said Father, "put the money in the box before we're tempted."

Mother's voice rose from the hatchway. "Is everybody hungry? Dinner's almost on the table."

"Come, let's run the boat ashore," said Father. "I don't want to be left up here by myself while the rest of you eat."

Chapter VI

DEAD MAN'S RIFFLE

FTER dinner the boys romped up and down the narrow deck with the dogs, while Susan washed the dishes. Just as she set the last iron pot on the stove to dry, she heard the blast of an unfamiliar horn and ran up to the roof to see what was happening.

A dark keelboat was skimming down the river with the brisk wind behind its square sail. The keelboatmen, in their gaudy red flannel shirts, blue jerkins and coonskin caps, lounged on the deck, playing with a pack of battered cards. One man was steering.

They began to sing hoarsely:

> Hard upon the beech oar!
> She moves too slow!
> All the way to Shawneetown,
> Long time ago!

"Hello, alligator-horses!" David called out shrilly. "Half horse, half alligator!"

The boatmen roared with laughter. "That's our name," one of them bellowed. "If you know anybody that wants a fight, we're spoiling for it. We're from Kentuck, and we're so tough that iron melts in our mouths."

"Keep to yourselves this time," Father shouted. "There's ladies aboard."

"That young one ain't no lady," another boatman bawled. "That's an angel!"

Susan blushed to the roots of her dark curls. Steve chuckled and gave her a dig in the ribs.

One of the boatmen leaped to his feet and pointed at Father.

"Suffering turnip seeds! If it ain't an optical pollution, that's George Doak without his red whiskers. The old goggled-eyed ring-tailed roarer!"

The rest of the crew cheered and waved their fur caps.

"Shut up, you son of a stuffed monkey," Father yelled good-naturedly.

The keelboat speedily left them behind, but the shouts continued until it sailed around a bend in the river.

"You know everybody on the river, don't you, Father?" said David admiringly.

"Hardly, Bub. But a flatboat man sometimes collides with the keelboatmen in the river towns."

"Did you ever fight with them?"

"Well, don't tell your mother, Bub, but there's times when a rough-and-tumble is the only path out of the wilderness."

"My peace-loving husband!" Mother's voice floated out through an open window.

Father grinned. "I don't fight when your mother's around. I've got religion now."

Steve hitched over to the center of the roof to rest his back against one of the rain barrels. "Did you ever wear the feather in your cap, Father?"

"What does that mean?" asked Susan.

Steve and David groaned.

"What on earth do girls talk about, anyway?" said Steve. "Why, when a boatman has licked his whole crew he can wear a red feather in his cap."

"Oh," said Susan. "Did any of those keelboatmen wear a feather?"

"No," said Steve promptly.

"Did you ever wear the feather, Father?" she asked.

"Feather-father, feather-father," David chanted. "That's very funny. Feather-father."

"Did you, Father?"

Father smiled reminiscently. "Once, on my second trip down the river. I had a gang of cutthroats for a crew, headed by a bandy-legged bully. He claimed I had promised them a whole gallon of rum a day throughout the trip. So I had to lick the lot of them."

David's mouth dropped open. "I wish I'd been there. I would have helped you."

"You were a baby in arms then, Bub."

"Well, anyway, I would now. Father, do you reckon you could buy me a coonskin cap like the ones the alligator-horses wear?"

"I'll see," Father promised.

"I wouldn't mind having one too," said Steve. "These woolen caps look silly on the river."

Father took one hand off the steering oar to rub his eyes.

"I'm getting groggy from watching the river too long. Will you take the oar a while, Red? And, Davie, you sit down at the bows and watch for snags. I'm going to take a nap."

"I think I'll go below and look over the account books," Susan said, "unless the boys need me."

"All right, come along."

Father paused halfway down the hatch. "Look out for Dead Man's Riffle somewhere along this winding stretch. You'll see the island, and you'll recognize the riffle by the churning of the waters. We shouldn't have any trouble in high water, but you'd better call me."

"All right, Father." Steve's eyes shone. "This is fun."

David walked forward and sat down beside the short flagstaff, swinging his feet over the edge of the roof. Bessie clumped across her pen and licked his shoes with her rough tongue. One of the geese spread her white wings and hissed. Now and then the yellow flag brushed against his tousled sandy hair.

"Steve, what would you do if a steamboat came round the bend?"

"I reckon I'd holler for Father. They stir up the water something terrible."

Steve planted his feet wide apart and gave the steering oar a slight twist to see how it felt. The boat creaked and started to swing. He hastily righted the oar and she straightened again.

"What happened?" David asked.

"I was just trying her out."

"You'd better not. Something might happen and Father would be mad."

"I can handle her, no matter what happens. The current carries her along."

"Steve, where do you suppose the 'Oliver Evans' is now?"

"You mean the 'Constitution.' She'd be halfway from Louisville to New Orleans by now. But I wouldn't be surprised to see her grounded somewhere. Her keel's too deep."

The storeboat rounded another turn.

David sat up straight. "Isn't—isn't that an island ahead? The water looks rough."

"I guess that's old Dead Man's Island, all right. Watch me take her down the riffle all by myself."

"Steve! You'd better not. I'm going to call Father."

"Baby! Watch me and you'll find out how to handle a boat."

David flung a look at Steve's freckled face, braced himself on the edge of the roof, and watched the island approaching.

Steve gritted his teeth and steered for the channel which led past the island. When the storeboat reached the riffle she seemed to leap forward. He turned pale and took a firmer grip on the steering oar. He glued his eyes to the waters ahead, looking for the smooth streak that indicated the channel. The oar turned itself in his hands as he let the boat follow the twisting path.

David clung to the flagstaff and began to whimper. Bessie gave a disturbed moo and rolled her soft red-brown eyes. Down below, the dogs whined and crockery rattled on the shelves. The little kitchen door opened against Bessie's flank, and Mother looked up at David.

"What's the matter? Why—" She gasped and steadied herself against the doorframe. Then she lowered her voice. "Be quiet, Davie boy. Don't upset Steve now. He may make out, the little blockhead. Why didn't you call your father?"

At last the island was behind them. As suddenly as the

current had laid hold of the boat, it released her to float quietly once more.

Mother blew a sigh of relief and went back into the kitchen. David let go of the flagstaff and sat up.

Steve relaxed his hold on the oar, and found that his hands were numb and his shoulders ached. His knees began to tremble. Then he noticed Susan's bright brown eyes watching him from the hatchway.

"Here, take the oar," he said desperately.

She ran up the ladder and took his place. "I would have waked Father if you'd had any trouble," she said quietly.

He grinned weakly and sat down on the roof. "I thought I'd be so smart. I wonder what Father will say."

Suddenly David shrieked. "Look out! There's a mark on the water ahead. Maybe it's a rock."

Steve jumped up and took the steering oar out of Susan's hands. "It couldn't be a rock. The water's too high. Oh!"

Something raked the bottom of the boat along her entire length. The stern rose a little, and the rain barrels slid toward the bows. Down below there was a clatter of falling pots and pans. The animals set up a commotion—barking, mooing, cackling, honking. Then the boat settled back and remained there.

Father came running up the ladder, rubbing his eyes. "What's all this?"

Steve was still clinging to the handle of the oar. "I guess we're grounded, Father," he said in a small voice.

Father looked around and blinked. "Why, we've passed the riffle! How—why, you flea-bitten little idiot! Do you mean to tell me you brought her down the riffle?"

"Yes, sir, I guess so."

Father took out his faded blue bandanna and mopped his forehead.

"We ought to get down on our knees and thank God," he said. "If the wind had shifted against you, or if you'd been a little stronger on the oar, you couldn't have done it."

"I guess I deserve a licking, sir."

"I want you to look back there at the riffle," said Father. "Do you see those dark spots under the water? Rocks. Last summer I saw a storeboat grounded near the left bank. They had to carry everything in the boat to shore, and it took them two days to mend the keel. Now do you see why I asked you to call me?"

"Yes, sir. I guess I just wanted to show you I could handle a boat. But I reckon we're stuck on a rock now."

"There's no rock here," said Father.

"Whatever it is," said Susan earnestly, "it's all my fault."

"I saw something," David put in excitedly, "and I hollered."

"Dave and Susan ain't to blame," said Steve. "I had the oar at the time."

"I didn't give it back to him soon enough, Father," Susan insisted. "That's why it's my fault."

Mother spoke up from the hatchway. "Why not finish the argument afterward? I need help down here. Brownie and Patch are doing the best they can, lapping up the broken eggs, but they refuse to use the mop."

"We'll be with you in a minute, Miss Biddy," said Father. "Now let's find out what's wrong before we spring a leak. Stand to your oar, Stevie. Don't let the current swing her about. Susan, jump down there in the pen and help out with the gouger. Dave, you and I will take the canoe and paddle around till we find out what's holding us."

When they had paddled halfway down the length of the boat Father pointed.

"There it is."

"What is it?" Mother called from the window.

"A sawyer—a tree brought down by high water, with its roots caught in the bed of the river. The trunk rises and falls with the current, so sometimes you're on it before you can see it."

"I didn't see anything but a mark on the water," David said.

"Don't worry about it, Bub. Sometimes you can't even see that much."

"What do we have to do, Father?" Steve asked. "Dive down and saw off the tree?"

Father peered down through the water. "It looks like a lucky chance for us. The top of the tree is pointing downstream. I reckon we could heave off if we could touch bottom with the sweeps."

He paddled back to the stern, and he and David hoisted the canoe to its usual place on the deck.

Father plunged one of the sweeps into the water and groped for the bottom. Finally he located an imbedded rock, and leaned his entire weight against the sweep. The boat scraped, swung in an arc, and floated free.

"Straighten her!" Father yelled. "That's right."

"Hurray! Hurray!"

"I'll take the steering oar now," said Father. "Steve, you look green about the gills. You'd better go below and help your mother pick up the pieces. We've had two narrow escapes."

"I'll never do a thing like that again," said Steve, as he stumbled down the hatchway.

"I'm willing to lay a bet on it," said Father. "But at times I wish we had another boatman aboard."

Chapter VII

OLD PAPPY

H ARDLY had Steve's red head disappeared through
the open trap door, than the gay strains of a fiddle
floated down the river. Father patted time with his
foot while he stood at the oar, and David got up and began
to jig. Susan clapped the rhythm for them.

A crude raft with a shed in the middle was gaining on the
storeboat, with two rough-looking men at the oars. The
fiddler, a wiry white-haired old man, sat in a chair in the
doorway of the shed, keeping time with his head and one
foot as he played.

When the raft drew near the storeboat, the fiddler waved
his bow and hallooed.

"George Doak, you old son of a stuffed alligator!"

Father let out a whoop. "Pappy! You walleyed old
caterpillar, where do you think you're bound?"

"Ain't bound nowhere, George. Just a-traveling." He
began to play another lively air.

"Stop that racket a minute, Pappy. You're the very man
I want to see. Do you want to work like an honest man?"

Pappy squinted up at him. "If there's no way out of
it, George."

"Jump on board then. We need another hand."

The old man said something to the two burly oarsmen,

and they nodded and steered the raft nearer the store-boat.

"Wait till I get my plunder, George."

Pappy dived into the shed and came out with a bundle wrapped in a red bandanna handkerchief. Without waiting for a helping hand he sprang on board.

"Steve," Father called down the hatch, "come here as fast as you can."

The boy's head appeared above the hatchway just as Pappy hoisted himself to the roof.

"That's my son Steve, Pappy, this young lady is Susan, and here's my David. Here, Steve, take the oar a while. Pappy's our new crew and I want to show him the outfit."

Steve hesitated. "Is it because you're disappointed in me, Father?"

Father punched him playfully with his fist. "Nonsense, Red. We need Pappy. He's as lively as a cricket in a hot frying pan, and I know you'll all like him."

"Some folks don't like me, but everybody likes my Katy," said Pappy, patting his fiddle.

Susan stepped up and held out her hand. "I think we're going to like both you and Katy."

"So do I," the boys chorused.

Pappy hitched up his loose brown pantaloons. "Well, George," he drawled, "if you was to pick out a family one by one, I don't see how you could do no better. Is your old woman aboard too?"

"Come on down below and see her. We'll dicker about your wages, and I'll tell you how we happen to be traveling in such style."

"I ain't exactly dressed for ladies," Pappy said ruefully,

looking down at his tattered blue jerkin, faded red woolen shirt, and flapping pantaloons.

"Miss Biddy won't care," said Father, and they climbed down the hatchway.

Mother welcomed Pappy cordially. "We're mighty glad to have you join us, Mr.—"

"It's an honor, ma'am. Just call me Pappy or Old Pap. I don't need no other name. Got no kinfolks, lost my family twenty-five years ago in an Indian raid. I've had too dang much trouble in my life to want to hang on to all my names." He smiled cheerfully.

From the shore came the faint sound of a planter's horn calling the family to supper. There was a loud answering blast from the storeboat's horn on the roof.

"Come on, Pappy," said Father. "We'll have to run the boat ashore to raise a little cash."

Two backwoodsmen in homespun and moccasins came on board, with their wives trailing behind them. The older of the men announced that he only wanted to buy a gunstock and a broadax. The other man and the two women walked around the store, silently looking over the stock.

But when Pappy began to play a tune on Katy, their eyes lighted up and the younger man broke into a jig. Mother grabbed a tin pot and beat time upon it, while the others clapped their hands.

Finally one of the wives said, "If we don't get back to our supper mighty soon, the younger ones will eat up all the vittles."

The dancing stopped, but the visitors had decided that they needed much more than a gunstock and broadax. After a great deal of dickering, they added a saddle, a pair of

scissors, two needles, two fishhooks, ten yards of printed chintz, and a frying pan.

In return, Father received all the money they had, and also a quantity of dried corn blades for the cow, shelled corn, a bag of wheat flour, a flitch of bacon, a bushel of potatoes, two pairs of moccasins and the promised coonskin caps for the boys.

"I'll have to help you with the accounts this time, Susan," said Father as they pushed off from the shore. "We have to set a price on what we use ourselves, and pay into the money box. What we don't use, we'll sell at the highest price in the big towns."

The storeboat floated only a mile or so farther before the sun began to sink behind the rosy clouds. David helped Pappy lash the boat to shore for the night and lingered a while on the roof to watch the changing sunset.

"I'll be blamed if I don't think we're tolerably near White's tavern," Pappy remarked. "I wish Mr. White could smell Miss Biddy's ham and eggs and fried potatoes and biscuits. If we was to stop at his tavern he'd give us nothing but sour bread and salt mutton, with a beaker of whiskey to wash it down."

Even the boys could not keep up with Pappy's appetite at the supper table. Long after the sunset had faded and white mists had begun to gather in the meadows, Pappy was still plunging his knife into the jar of apple butter. Finally he moved his chair away from the table with a sigh of contentment, and reached for Katy.

While Susan and the boys cleared away the table and washed the dishes, he sang in his drawling voice:

It's oh! as I was a-walking out,
    One morning in July,
I met a maid who axed my trade—
    Says I, I'll tell you presently,
    Miss, I'll tell you presently.
And it's oh! she was so neat a maid,
    That her stockings and her shoes
She toted in her lily white hands
    For to keep them from the dews.

Now and then Father added his deep bass, singing "tra, la, la" whenever he forgot the words.

Mother interrupted to hold a consultation about where Pappy was to sleep.

"Don't go to no trouble about me," the old man protested. "I wasn't raised a pet."

"It's no trouble," Mother assured him. "We have an extra featherbed and plenty of sheets and quilts. We can make up your bed in the store. In the daytime we can roll them up and put them in our cabin."

"Don't that beat the Dutch!" said Pappy. "Sheets, after all these years!"

He wagged his head and swung into another tune.

Although they did not want to leave the music, the young people soon began to yawn, and Mother sent them to bed. Through the thin partition they could still hear the old melodies that Katy was singing.

"Oh, my," said Susan sleepily, burrowing deeper under the covers, "can you believe we were in Pittsburgh only this morning? And isn't it fun to have Pappy aboard?"

The two boys were already asleep.

Chapter VIII

MOSTLY CONVERSATION

THE next day, while the storeboat floated through the gray morning mist, Mother began the lessons. They could hear voices overhead, and occasionally a burst of laughter from Pappy and Father. But Mother ignored their fidgeting and made them all write the names of ten European countries and their capitals.

"It isn't fair, Mother," Susan burst out. "I finished geography two years ago."

Mother was firm. "Nobody ever finishes learning, Susan. It won't hurt you to go back. I noticed you had trouble remembering the capital of Denmark."

Steve looked up from his work. "Mother," he said earnestly, "I don't really think I ought to spend so much time studying. Father and Pappy must be tired by now. Don't you think I ought to go up and help them?"

Mother laughed aloud. "I think they can manage without you for a while. Nobody on this boat is allowed to play the truant. Now let's have a short spelling bee."

At last Mother released them. The boys grabbed their new coonskin caps and swarmed up the steps to the roof, followed by Susan. The bright morning sun had dispelled all the mist, and the air was even warmer than the day before.

"Oh, Father," cried David, "there's a cabin on the shore.

I'll wager you've passed lots of clearings already, because I wasn't here to blow the horn."

"Tarnation!" said Father, shaking his head. "I always forget. Sound the trumpet, Gabriel."

David gave a long blast on the red horn, while Father and Pappy turned the storeboat toward the bank.

"Don't wear out that horn, Davie," warned Pappy, as he gave a twist to his sweep to speed the landing. "If you puff all the noise out of it, we'll have to get ahold of Mike Fink."

"Who's he?"

"Mike? Why, he's the greatest keelboatman on the river. He's a half horse, half alligator if there ever was one. We call him the Snapping Turkle because he's always ready to fight. He can outrun, outhop, outjump, throw down, drag out, and beat down the ears of any man in the country. He's chock full of fight, Mike is."

"But what about the horn?"

"Well, you see," Pappy drawled, "Mike can imitate anything he hears. Sometimes he gets to imitating wild critters, and pretty soon here come bears, buffalo and polecats licking his fingers and calling him Mammy."

"Oh, Pappy, what fibs!" Susan scolded.

"Nothing's fibs when you're talking about Mike Fink," said Pappy. "Now about that horn. You see, Mike never carries a horn, because he can toot better than any horn ever made. Matter of fact, I've seen many a horn turn red with mortification after hearing Mike toot."

"How can you explain our horn?" asked Steve, his eyes twinkling. "It's already red."

"Where did that horn come from?"

"Pittsburgh."

"So did Mike," said Pappy triumphantly. "You don't know what might have happened to that horn before you got ahold of it."

"Tell us more about Mike Fink," David begged.

Pappy shook his head. "Some other time," he said. "Here come some folks with money jingling in their pockets. I'll have to put Katy to work to charm it away from them."

In spite of this and three other stops at scattered farmhouses, the storeboat arrived at Legionsville shortly after the noonday dinner. The sound of the horn brought almost all the townspeople down to the landing. Susan was kept busy writing down small sales—a few sheets of pins, hooks and eyes, a penknife, spools of thread, essence of peppermint, and other inexpensive items.

Within an hour they had left the town and were headed downstream again.

"Legionsville," said Pappy slowly. "There's been changes since we camped there with Mad Anthony Wayne in 1792."

The young people sat down with their backs against the rain barrels and listened. Pappy settled down on the edge of the hatchway with his feet on the steps below.

" 'Twas just an outpost then," he said.

"Were you in the Indian wars, Pappy?" said David, with round eyes. "You must be awful old."

"It don't seem so long ago, Davie," said Pappy. "Yes, I thought it was my bounden duty to kill Injuns. They'd burned down my cabin and killed my family."

"Were you mean to them?" asked David. "Was that why they did it?"

"Hush, Davie," Susan said. "Maybe Pappy doesn't like to talk about it."

"That's all right, Miss Susie," Pappy reassured her. "It don't worry me no more. Well, I done nothing personal against the Injuns. But like a lot of others, I had an idea it was all right to pay Injuns a barrel of whiskey, a few laced coats and a pile of blankets for a parcel of land as big as two states. And don't let me catch them anywhere in the neighborhood. An Injun slinking around on white man's land made a mighty fine target for a rifle."

"General Harrison says we need soldiers to get control of the prairies in the far West," Steve said. "Do you believe that, Pappy?"

"Son, it's hard to say. Maybe it's too late now to try honest dealing with Injuns. But I sometimes get to wondering if we oughtn't to show a little more respect for them. Then they'd have more respect for us."

"Maybe General Harrison was thinking more about the English and the Spanish in the West," Susan remarked thoughtfully.

Pappy bristled. "Them foreigners better watch out. Some day we're going to need all that room. They got no rights here."

"Pappy," David said, "suppose you saw an Indian over there on the shore by that big oak tree. Would you kill him?"

Pappy shook his head. "Not unless he killed me first."

"Oh, now you're fooling me," said David, as the others laughed.

"Well," said Pappy, "I'd be inclined to ask him what he wanted. I've seen a lot of mighty civilized, friendly In juns. Down on the Mississippi they come down to the shore and help us chop wood, out of pure good nature."

"That's true," said Father at the steering oar. "The French seem to have set us a good example in fair dealing down that way."

David drew a deep breath. "When I was little," he said, "I used to want to be an Indian fighter. But now I've decided to be an alligator-horse."

The storeboat swung around a bend and came upon a large raft moored to the shore. It looked like a floating village. The hut in the middle was swarming with tow-headed children, and a woman was hanging out the family washing above the broad backs of a dozen sand-colored pigs. A mule peered around the corner of the hut and gave a loud heehaw. The children on the raft began to shout and dance.

Steve and David waved their coonskin caps. Brownie and Patch rushed up and down the deck and added their barks until the noise echoed from hill to hill.

Pappy cupped his hands and bellowed, "Hello, the pigsty! Think there's enough room in the West for all them critters?"

A bearded man chopping wood on the shore answered him. "If there's room enough for you there's room enough for my pigs!"

While the others laughed, old Pappy scratched his head. "If I had time I'd pin his ears back."

But the raft was soon left behind, and the dogs settled back on their haunches.

"So you want to be a keelboatman, Davie," Pappy remarked. "What about you, Steve?"

"Oh, I'm going to be a steamboat man."

"Was you folks in Pittsburgh in 1811 when the 'New Orleans' was built?"

"Oh, yes," said Steve. "I was only a little boy, but I remember when she left Pittsburgh. Mr. Nicholas Roosevelt took his wife with him, and they had a big dog."

"Well," said Pappy, "I was on the river that summer. I'll never forget when that thing came a-snorting round the bend. She churned the waters so she upset canoes and those hollowed-out logs they call pirogues. It was a caution."

"Was everybody surprised?" asked David.

Pappy whooped. "I'll never forget it. Some folks took to the woods, and others was too scared to run. Whenever she blew her whistle or let out a blast of steam, folks moaned and groaned and said the devil hisself was let loose, if you'll pardon the language."

"Oh, you're joking," Susan insisted.

"If it ain't true, may I be bit by an alligator tomorrow. Some thought the British was coming up the river, and ran for their muskets. Other folks was sure the comet of 1811 had fallen into the river. And when the 'New Orleans' met up with the earthquake down near New Madrid, everybody was satisfied there was a connection."

"Is he telling the truth, Father?" Susan asked.

"For once in his life," Father replied.

"Have you ever been on a steamboat, Pappy?" David asked. "Father has. He's been on lots of steamboats. He helped Captain Shreve run the blockade at New Orleans during the war."

"I know Henry Shreve mighty well," said Pappy. "He been on the river for pretty near eighteen years. About

your age when he started, Steve. Last year he let me ride
on the 'Washington' from Marietta to Gallipolis without
paying passage."

"How was it?" Steve asked eagerly.

"There's a real boat," said Pappy, smacking his lips. "And
there's a real man. George, did you know the Fulton
and Livingston company offered him hush money to stop
fighting their monopoly of the Western rivers?"

"I heard that," said Father. "They ought to know by
this time that Henry Shreve means what he says. Livingston
can threaten till the cows come home, but Shreve has made
up his mind that the Fulton patent is contrary to the prin-
ciples of liberty. He won't stop till every court in the country has ruled it out."

"Isn't the patent legal?" asked Steve. "Didn't Robert
Fulton invent the steamboat?"

"You've got the wrong sow by the ear, Steve," said Pappy.
"Fulton only proved it was practical."

"Didn't you ever hear of John Fitch, Steve?" Father
asked. "There's the man who invented the steamboat. He
made a successful trial on the Delaware more than twenty
years before Fulton's 'Clermont.' In 1791 he had his second
steamboat chugging around on Collect Pond, right there in
New York City. But he didn't have money enough to buy
a patent before his time limit expired."

"I didn't know that," said Steve in surprise. "I've heard
lots of river men say steamboats would be in common use
if they didn't have to pay so much to the Fulton and
Livingston company. I thought they were fighting the
price, not the right to the patent."

"Why does the law allow such a patent?" Susan asked indignantly.

"Sometimes," said Father thoughtfully, "there's a slight difference between the law and what we think is right. It comes from improper interpretation of the meaning of the law. But in this country we always have a chance to vote for the right laws, or for the right judges to interpret those laws."

"When Henry Shreve gets through with the cases against him and the 'Enterprise' and the 'Washington,'" said Pappy, "there won't be any Fulton and Livingston company. There'll be free navigation. There'll be so many steamboats crawling on the river that you can't get a pole between them."

"And they'll all be high-pressure engines and double-deckers like the 'Washington,'" Steve said.

"I shouldn't be surprised," Father agreed.

"Where's Captain Shreve now? Are they holding the 'Washington' until the case is settled?"

"Last I heard," said Father, "he threatened to sue Livingston for what he might lose if they held her. So the marshal released her and he sailed back up river. He was held up by low waters at Shippingport below Louisville."

"Wouldn't it be a good idea," said Steve, "if everybody organized something like a trade union against the Fulton and Livingston company? If nobody would work for them or ride on their boats, they'd have to give up their monopoly."

"I won't say it won't come to that," Pappy replied cautiously. "It does seem like Henry Shreve oughtn't to have to fight those polecats all by hisself. He don't care what happens to him so much. He just don't like a monopoly, and there's not a plain man on the river that ain't on his side. I don't say there ain't been no talk about trade unions on the river."

Father smiled. "Are you putting ideas into my children's heads, Pappy?"

"No, George," the old man drawled. "Just airing a few sentiments of me and you and Thomas Jefferson and the other great minds of America."

Chapter IX

RAIN

O N the third morning, the fog hung low and heavy. Somewhere to their left they heard a horn, the muffled splashing of poles, and the deep voice of a patroon calling, "Set!" "Lift!" "Set!"

Pappy blew the storeboat's horn as a warning, and was given an Indian war whoop for answer. For a moment they saw the faint dark outline of a keelboat, but it was gone as suddenly as it had appeared.

"There'll be no traveling for us until this fog lifts," said Father. "Pappy, you and I can rearrange the shelves in the store while the children have their lessons."

After a few hours the mist had risen to the tops of the rolling hills on each side of the river, and the budding trees were visible again. But the sky was overcast with dark clouds.

No sooner had David loosened the fasts than a cold rain began to fall. A stiff southwesterly wind blew up, whipping the river into whitecaps.

Pappy took the steering oar. "All the rest of you stay below where it's warm and dry," he said. "I'll holler if I need help."

The pelting rain drove against the pen at the front of the boat. The wet yellow flag flapped against its pole.

Pappy buttoned up his old blue jacket and tilted his coon-skin cap to keep the rain from blinding him.

Mother ran out into the pen and threw a piece of heavy brown homespun over Bessie, who stood in her shed twitching her skin when the water dripped on her flanks and trickled down her long nose. The chickens and geese had hopped up on their roosts beside her and fluffed their feathers to shed the raindrops.

Father closed the sliding trap door, and accompanied by Brownie and Patch, made a tour of the boat to see if there were any leaks in the roof.

"The boat's as fit as a fiddle," he finally reported.

"At any rate," said Mother, "the rain barrels will have a chance to fill."

Susan got out the set of jackstraws which Father had carved for them during one of his long trips. She made a little pile of the miniature wooden saws, shovels, axes, rifles, and brooms on the kitchen table, and she and the boys took turns trying to remove a single straw without moving any other in the pile. Everyone tried for the saw because it counted the most, but the gentle rocking of the boat shifted the jackstraws so often that it was hard to tell who won.

"Oh, this isn't much fun," Steve complained. "I'd rather read. Let's each get a book out of the store."

The three went in and looked over the shelves. Steve chose Sir Walter Scott's *Waverley* and David seized a copy of *Robinson Crusoe*.

"What are you going to read, Susan?" Steve asked.

"Shakespeare," she said, tucking a little volume under her arm.

"Which one?"

"Well, *Romeo and Juliet*."

"Oh, that's a silly one about love. You ought to read *Julius Caesar*," Steve said.

"Who's reading this book, you or me?" Susan tossed her curls.

"Oh, all right, all right. But you don't mind if it makes me sick, do you?"

"Not at all," she said with dignity. "I'm going to lie down on my bed and read by myself."

"Sorry," said Steve with a grin, "but I'm going to make myself comfortable on my own bed right next to you."

"So am I," said David. "I like to lie on my stomach and read."

"Oh, dear," Susan groaned, "that's what it is to have brothers. No peace."

Steve gave her a brotherly shove into the little room. "Mind you keep quiet now," he said. "I don't wish to be disturbed."

At length they heard a roar from Pappy on the roof. "Somebody come up and help me run ashore."

Father climbed up, and a few minutes later the storeboat jarred against the muddy bank.

Pappy came into the kitchen drenched and shivering. The young people left their books and came in as Mother was helping him remove his jerkin.

"It's getting as dark as a stack of black cats outside," he said. "I got the delicate blue devils looking at them whitecaps, if you'll pardon the language."

Mother made him change to some of Father's dry clothes, which hung in loose folds on his thin frame. She draped

his wet pantaloons and jerkin over a chair near the stove
to dry while she fixed dinner.

After dinner Pappy tried to play a tune, but the long
sleeves of Father's jacket got in his way and would not
stay rolled up.

"Well," he drawled, "I reckon I can't do nothing but
talk in these duds."

"Tell us about Mike Fink," David demanded.

"Did you ever hear about the time Mike got arrested?
Well, seems he run afoul of the law just once or twice too
often down toward Louisville and there was a reward out
for him. Old friend of Mike's which happened to be a constable thought he'd admire to collect that reward.

"So next time Mike hove to at Louisville this here constable met him with a long face.

" 'Mike,' he says, 'I shore hate to tell you, knowing you
got feelings against it, but I got to arrest you.'

" 'Not me,' says Mike. 'I don't aim to get throwed in
jail.'

" 'Now, Mike,' says the constable, " 'tain't a question of
jail. It's just a little matter of going to the courthouse long
enough for me to collect my reward. I need that money
powerful bad, because my six little chillen ain't got no shoes.'

"Mike he's so kind-hearted that when he thought of them
little chillen without no shoes, he begun to wipe his eyes and
blow his nose. The constable he blubbered into his bandanna and first thing you knowed Mike's whole crew was
a-hollering and bawling.

" 'Well,' says Mike, 'seeing as it won't do me no harm and
long as you're an old friend, I'll let you arrest me, but only
on one condition.'

" 'I'll do anything for an old friend,' says the constable and he wipes his eyes.

" 'I'll go with you to the courthouse,' says Mike, 'if you'll let me travel on my boat with my whole crew. I don't feel exactly easy on dry land.'

" 'It ain't possible,' says the constable, 'because the courthouse is way up on the hill. I reckon my six little chillen'll have to go without shoes all their lives. Good-by, Mike,' he says, very sad.

" 'Hold on,' says Mike. 'A boat's a boat, even if she's on wheels. Fetch me a wagon and a team of oxen.'

"So the constable got a wagon and a team, and they loaded the boat on the wagon.

" 'Stand by with your poles!' says Mike to his crew. 'We may strike a riffle.'

"The boatmen whooped and Mike tooted like a boat horn, and them oxen hauled them up Third Street. Halfway up the hill, Mike scratched his head and then let out a yell: 'Set poles!'

"The crew set their poles in the mud.

" 'Back her!' says Mike.

"The men heaved and shoved on their poles and they went sliding back downhill, oxen and all. The constable he trotted after. 'What's the matter, Mike?' says he.

" 'Well,' says Mike, 'I got to thinking about jail again.'

" 'You got no cause to worry,' says the constable. 'Ain't you got no feelings about my six little chillen?'

"Mike scratched his head again. 'You're sure the law's on my side?'

" 'Bound to be,' says the constable.

"So he whacked the oxen and they started back up the

hill. This time they got to the top and Mike was took into the courtroom with the crew following after. There was a big crowd waiting to testify that Mike had been a nuisance since the day he was born. But seems like nobody had any proof of it, short of a few busted noses left over from one fight or another.

"After a heap of talk the judge banged on the table and says, 'Case dismissed! Insufficient evidence.'

" 'If it pleases your honor,' somebody speaks up, 'you ain't give me no chance to bring up the question of Mr. Fink shooting out all the candles in my tavern.'

" 'Ain't you heard the judge?' Mike yells. 'To your posts, mannies!'

"Mike and his men took one jump through the courtroom window smack into their boat, and them poor old oxen was so surprised they slid backwards all the way down to the river. And Mike he ain't set foot in Louisville since."

"Is that a true story?" asked David.

Pappy tried once more to roll up the long sleeves of Father's jacket. "I'm satisfied it's true," he said solemnly. "I saw the wagon tracks with my own eyes."

Mother looked up from her darning. "George, did you ever meet this wonderful Mike Fink?" she asked.

"Well," said Father, "once I passed Covington just after Mike and his men had broken up a militia drill. The streets were littered with pieces of blue uniforms, brass buttons and trampled cocked hats."

"Why didn't the soldiers shoot Mike?" asked David.

"Well, I reckon they didn't consider it war," said Father. "You can't shoot a man down because he wants to play."

"Did you see Mike himself, Father?" Steve asked.

"Not that day. By the time I came along he and his men were half a mile down river, and the fife and drum were calling the militia back to drill. But I did see Mike once in Natchez-under-the-hill."

"What was he up to?" asked Pappy. "That's a town after Mike's own heart."

"Oh, it was one of his Saturday night jokes. Two of his boatmen stretched a rope across the street, and Mike and the rest of the crew were whooping and hollering and chasing folks down that way to see them fall over the rope. I watched them from a dark alley. Pretty soon the sheriff came along and ran the whole crew back to their boat."

"That must have been fun," David said, his eyes sparkling.

"Fun for Mike," said Mother grimly. She laid aside her darning and went to the window. "I do believe the rain has stopped."

"Pappy, see if your clothes are dry," Father suggested. "We want to get a little piece on our way before dark. This is a wild and dreary spot to spend the night."

Chapter **X**

GOOD-BY TO PENNSYLVANIA

THE rain continued intermittently for several days in gentle showers that did not hinder the progress of the storeboat or keep the settlers away when the boat made a landing.

By this time the Doaks felt as though they had always lived on a storeboat. They grew accustomed to the sounds and smells of the river, and no longer noticed the motion of the boat. Occasionally they heard the crack of a rifle in the hills. Once a deer crashed through the brush on the shore and came to a stop, one forefoot raised, ears forward, snuffing the breeze. Then he wheeled and bounded away into the forest.

The daily chores and lessons went on without interruption except when there were customers on board. Steve and Susan took turns with the milking, the churning of the butter, and the scrubbing. David wiped dishes, kept the pewter polished, and saw that all the shelves were dusted every day. Sometimes Pappy helped with the chores, or insisted upon milking red Bessie.

"I have to keep my hand in," he said.

Every other day, the men and boys went ashore to hunt in the woods for a fallen hickory or ash tree, which made the best firewood. After chopping the big timber into stove lengths, they gathered the chips into baskets to use for kindling. From time to time they carried wooden buckets ashore and filled them with well water for drinking.

Sometimes between showers they saw women washing clothes in big kettles on the banks of the river, where there was plenty of driftwood to build a fire.

One warm day they came upon four little boys swimming in the river. David and Steve set up a howl until Mother promised that henceforth they might go swimming every Saturday afternoon instead of bathing in the wooden tub.

"I wish I knew how to swim, even if it isn't ladylike," Susan sighed.

"I'd be disappointed if you were too ladylike, my dear," said Mother. "We have only one life to live, and it seems a pity to be hampered by gentility. I've got no objection to your learning to swim, though not in the Ohio river."

Father bought two fishhooks and two lengths of strong silk fishline from the storeboat and weighted them with lead bullets. The boys baited the hooks with bacon rind and let the lines trail in the water at the stern. After half an hour without even a strike, Steve grew impatient, but David persevered.

While he was watching Steve haul in his line and wind it around a stick, there was a jerk on his own line. Instinctively he gripped the cord tighter in his fist.

"I've got a bite!" he shouted.

"Pull in your line!" said Father.

David pulled, but there was a more violent tug at the other end. His feet slipped, he lost his balance and tumbled into the river.

Father, at the steering oar, shouted with laughter and called down, "Chase him, Bub!"

Mother came running up the steps of the hatchway. "Am I missing something?"

Still guffawing, the others pointed to David floundering in the water.

"Laws!" Mother cried. "Why doesn't somebody save him?"

"He can swim as well as that fish," said Father. "Watch him."

In a few minutes David clambered back on the boat, sputtering and shaking the water out of his sandy hair, but still holding the line.

"I'll hold your feet so you won't slip," offered Steve. "Pull him in."

After a struggle, David drew in the line and flopped a big fish on the deck beside him, where it continued to thrash. It was black with a blue-white belly.

"That's a catfish. Don't let him stick you," Father cautioned. "He's a fine chunk of a fellow."

"Well, I guess we'll have fried fish for dinner," said Mother. "But it seems to me more trouble than it's worth. Come on down and change your wet clothes, Davie."

After that, David could generally be found trailing a line over the stern. And since most of the fish in the river were large and full of battle, he often lost in the first struggle. Whenever the family heard a whoop and a splash, they smiled and nodded.

"Another big fish has caught Davie," Mother would remark, and step over to the chair beside the stove to see if his other clothes were dry yet.

By Sunday, the thirtieth of March, the rainy spell was over. The sun shone again on the river and there was a fresh woodsy smell in the air. The willows that dipped their branches into the water along the river's edge were faintly green, the beeches were budding, and new grass was beginning to shoot up along the banks.

Since it was Sunday, there were few sounds on the river. They could even hear hogs grunting in the woods and cowbells tinkling in remote pastures. An occasional raft loaded with timber or flour disturbed the quiet for a few minutes. And sometimes the smell of salt fish announced the approach of a raft from New York state.

When the rooster crowed or the hens cackled with pride at having laid an egg, Pappy leaned over the edge of the roof to shake his finger at them.

"Don't you know it's Sunday, you sassy birds?"

Now and then they heard the settlers singing hymns in their isolated cabins. Once they passed a little unpainted meetinghouse, where the singing was much louder. Outside under the trees, saddle horses and teams waited patiently and switched their long tails at the flies. From the meetinghouse, wagon trails and footpaths branched out in all directions through the woods. Three or four skiffs were tied on the bank.

"I don't see any houses near the meetinghouse," Susan remarked. "Why did they build it way off in the woods?"

"Well," Father explained, "there aren't enough preachers in the West to go around. So instead of a meetinghouse in every settlement, they build the church where it can be reached by as many folks as possible."

"But where's the preacher's house?" she asked.

"He's probably a circuit-rider. Preaches here one Sunday, somewhere else next Sunday."

"It must keep him busy just riding from one church to another."

"Well, some folks may have ridden all night to hear him preach."

Father and Pappy made a landing shortly after noon, and they all sat down to dinner together. They had fried chicken and apple pie, because Father had accepted two chickens and some dried apples as part payment for a sheet of pins, some peppermint and bitters, leather shoestrings, a wooden bucket and a tin dipper.

After dinner Mother read aloud several chapters of the Bible, and they sang a few hymns, with accompaniment by Katy.

"I never tried to play hymns before," said Pappy jubilantly. "Some folks say the Lord don't like to hear nothing but hymns, but I always say He wouldn't have allowed mankind to invent the fiddle if he'd mistrusted a good reel or a hoe-down."

On Monday the storeboat arrived at the little town of Beaver, built high on the right bank at the foot of Beaver Creek. David blew the horn, while Steve stood ready to make the boat fast to shore beside two empty skiffs. Susan was below, getting out the money box and the account books from their hiding place in Father's room.

As they watched a group of chattering women with market baskets file down the steep path to the landing, Pappy remarked sourly, "I don't think very highly of this town."

"Why not?" Father inquired. "There's a good printing office, a post office, and several tolerably good stores."

"Worst jail in Pennsylvania," said Pappy.

"How do you know, Pappy?" asked Steve, grinning.

"Well, Red, don't tell your mother, but I been in it. One night about two years ago here in Beaver a keelboatman by the name of Wilkins come into the tavern and dared me to drink a pint of rum right off, without stopping for breath."

"Did you do it?"

"I did, because I don't like to take a dare," said Pappy. "Besides, he wore the feather in his cap."

"What happened?"

"Well, seems I felt like a wildcat and I lit into him. After he come to, he got the sheriff after me and they put me in jail. That just ain't honorable. I'm still a-looking for him. I may be old, but I'm spry, and I can outbutt and outkick any man but Mike Fink."

"Where was he from?" asked Father.

"Kentuck. He's a bad one and as crooked as a barrelful of snakes."

The first customers had climbed on board, and Father escorted them down into the store. Pappy touched his bow to the resin and tightened Katy's strings. After he had played a while, the women in the store bought so much that they had to take off their sunbonnets to hold the overflow from the market baskets.

It was afternoon before the Doaks had time to eat their midday dinner, and the sky was beginning to redden before the accounts were added up and the shelves of the store put in order again. Meantime a keelboat headed upstream had glided into the eddy beside them. The entire crew in their bright blue jackets had tumbled off their boat and climbed up the steep bank, singing and shouting.

"We might as well stop here for the night," said Father.

"The good ladies of Beaver seem to prefer our stock to what they see in their stores, and they may have some money left."

"In that case," Pappy ventured, "I might go ashore to-night to find out the news from down river."

"Look out for those keelboatmen," Father warned, "and don't take any dares."

"And be sure to keep out of jail," Steve added. Then he clapped his hand over his mouth. "Oh! I forgot! You said not to tell Mother."

Mother smiled. "Pappy told me about the Beaver jail one night after you children were asleep."

Pappy grinned sheepishly. "It's just a manner of speaking, when I say don't tell your mother."

The next morning the eggs and bacon were cold before Pappy appeared in the kitchen doorway.

David looked up and shouted, "Pappy has a black eye!"

"Is that polite?" chided Mother, although she joined in the laughter.

Pappy sat down at the table heavily. "Seems like I got a touch of the rheumatism too."

"You didn't happen to run down your friend Wilkins, did you, Pappy?" Father asked, passing his cup for more coffee.

"No, but he ain't the only two-legged varmint trying to pass hisself off as a man."

The young people leaned forward eagerly, but Father only asked calmly, "What was the news?"

"Well," Pappy drawled between mouthfuls, "I heard Captain Shreve left Shippingport for New Orleans early this month."

"With the 'Washington'?" Steve put in.

"That's right. And a certain snaggle-toothed individual who calls hisself a keelboatman says the 'Washington' will never make the Falls coming back up river."

"Oh, he's wrong," said Steve hotly. "Captain Shreve did it with the 'Enterprise,' and the 'Washington' is a much better boat."

"Well," continued Pappy, "I asked him kindly why Henry Shreve built a flat-bottom boat, if it wasn't so's she could travel over little riffles like the Falls."

"The Falls aren't exactly riffles, Pappy," Father interposed.

"They's riffles to the 'Washington,'" Pappy insisted. "And then I asked him politely why Captain Shreve built a steam engine with more power to it than the contraptions previously known to man, if it wasn't for the sake of uphill going."

Steve beamed. "What did he say then, Pappy?"

"Well, his arguments was waterlogged. So he poked my eye, and I poked his eye. Then he kicked me, and I kicked him. He butted me in the stomach, and I got up and butted him in the stomach. Then he got up and hit my ear, and I hit his ear."

Pappy stopped to rub his swollen left ear thoughtfully.

"So then he hit me in the eye, and I hit him in the eye. He knocked me down, and about that time I began to get mad. So I knocked him down."

"What did he do then?" David leaned his elbows on the table.

"Well, his friends carried him back to the keelboat, I

guess," said Pappy modestly. "Good riddance to bad rub-
bidge, I says."

"How did you happen to get back to the boat without
help—or did you?" said Father.

"Well, I had help in a way," Pappy said. "They told me
the sheriff was coming, and first thing I knew I was back
here and had the trap door locked."

"Look outside, Davie, and see if that keelboat is still
here," Mother said anxiously.

"I already looked," said Pappy. "Must have left with the
full moon along about three or four o'clock."

"Thank heaven," said Mother.

"But the sheriff is still in Beaver," said Pappy.

"In that case," said Father, "we might as well cast off."

"I was coming to that," said Pappy mildly. "He's a
nosy man."

In a jiffy the fasts were loosened and the storeboat was
on its way. As the town receded, they heard a shout from
the shore. A man was scrambling down the bank, shaking
his fist.

Pappy waved his fur cap. "Good-by, sheriff! Sorry we
can't stay no longer."

Mother poked her head out. "George, doesn't it seem a
little disrespectful of the law to run away like this?"

Father laughed. "Now, Miss Biddy, the sheriff is probably glad Pappy got away. Remember he'd have to feed
Pappy in the jail."

"Well," said Mother, slightly relieved, "it didn't seem exactly practical to wait around in Beaver until he got out.
Come along, children. It's lesson time."

All day they floated between green sloping banks. Over-

head the clouds drifted like wisps of wool across the clear
blue sky. During the day they made nine brief stops at
farmhouses and taverns, and finally lay by for the night at
the little settlement of Georgetown on the left bank.

"No going ashore tonight, Pappy," Father announced.

"There's more taverns than houses in Georgetown,"
Pappy wheedled. "Hear the tavern signs a-creaking in the
wind? Don't that make you want to let me go ashore?"

"No," said Father firmly.

Pappy looked longingly toward the village, but followed
Father down the hatchway. After supper, while Pappy was
tuning his fiddle, Father remarked, "Tomorrow morning
we'll be traveling between Ohio on one side and Virginia *
on the other."

"I'd like to catch a fish right on the state line," David
said. "Show it to me when we get there, Father."

"Well, I don't know that you can see the state line, Bub,
but I'll tell you when we get there."

"Oh," said David. "I thought it was marked, like the
map."

Before they had finished breakfast the next morning, customers began to pile into the storeboat and Father did a sur-
prising amount of trade.

"I wouldn't have thought there was so much money in
Georgetown," Mother said afterward.

"It's the weather," said Father. "During a damp spell the
Georgetown folks sell lots of rock oil for rheumatism, and
they can't find enough to buy in the local dry goods store."

"I ought to lay in a bottle of rock oil myself," said
Pappy.

* Now West Virginia.

"In low water," Father continued, "you can smell the oil for miles."

"Unless there's a cargo of dried fish going by," Pappy added.

Barely half an hour after they left Georgetown, Father yelled, "Mill Creek Island! We're passing the state line!"

The young people left their geography lesson and scampered up the hatchway. David jumped down to the deck and threw out his fishline.

"Don't hurry, Father," he called excitedly.

"Ohio on your right and Virginia on your left," Father proclaimed with a sweeping gesture. "Good-by to Pennsylvania!"

Steve whooped and threw his cap into the air. The wind caught it and wafted it back beyond the boat. He turned and ruefully watched it land, fur side up, just beyond David's line.

"Don't do that, Steve," David grumbled. "You'll scare the fish."

"Sorry," Steve said, tearing off his jacket and moccasins. "Can't lose my cap."

He took a running dive and shot into the water with hardly a splash. In a moment he came up puffing and blowing and swam after his cap with flaying arms.

A raft piled high with logs bore down on him, pulled by six oarsmen. Steve gripped his cap with his teeth like a dog and swam back to the boat.

"That ain't no alligator-horse," a boatman yelled. "That's a water spaniel!"

Steve clambered aboard the storeboat and waved derisively. The oarsmen grinned and continued to ply their oars.

"Hello, the raft!" Father shouted. "Where are you from?"

"Olean, New York."

"Where are you bound?"

"New Orleans."

"Give Captain Shreve my respects," called Steve, who was beginning to shiver in his dripping pantaloons and shirt.

"Who's he?" The question floated back to him.

A roar of rage came from Pappy. "Son of a stuffed red-headed peckerwood!" he bellowed after the raft. "Go back to Olean till you learn something!"

Then David caught his fish and fell overboard with it. He scrambled back aboard the boat and held up a perch still flopping on the hook.

"See, Father? It's not very big, but I caught it almost on the state line. I would have caught it right on the line if it hadn't been for Steve's cap and the raft."

"That's a might fine minnow, Bub. I believe you fell in the water by force of habit. Now both you boys run down below and change your clothes before you catch your death."

Mother threw up her hands when the two dripping boys trailed into the kitchen.

"I knew there was a reason for not doing the washing Monday," she said. "If I put it off much longer, you'll wash all your own clothes in the river. Bub, will you put a bar of soap in your pocket the next time you fish?"

The boys giggled and rummaged in the chest for clean clothes.

"If it keeps on getting warm we can dry off in the sun," said Steve.

"Or better still," said Mother, "you can leave off clothes entirely, like the little boys in the backwoods."

"Mother!" David reddened to the ears. "With people around?"

But Steve laughed. "You're glad to be out of the city, ain't you, Mother?"

"Yes, I am, Stevie. I'm well satisfied to keep my blue bombazine and the green poplin dress in the chest. They may be stylish, but I don't care to climb ladders in them."

"Ladies' clothes must be awful," said David. "I'm glad I'm a boy."

Chapter XI

SIMON

SPRING was well along by now. The forests were bursting into leaf, and the breezes carried the fragrance of the peach trees blossoming in many a clearing. All the farmers were out in their freshly plowed fields, and Father did a brisk trade in plow-irons and hoes.

The featherbeds were too warm for the sweet-smelling nights, and so they were rolled up, tied, and stacked in a corner of Father's cabin. Susan found them an excellent hiding place for the money box every night.

The boys and men laid aside their heavy clothes and coon-skin caps for the summer and changed to blue jean pantaloons and bright figured calico shirts. Susan began to look longingly at a little straw poke bonnet in the store, trimmed with flowers and ribbons to tie under the chin.

"I know I'll never own such a bonnet," she sighed, "but I can't help wanting it."

"Why don't you make a bonnet for yourself out of plaited grasses?" Mother suggested.

"I never thought of that!" Susan exclaimed.

After that, she went ashore at every landing to gather grasses, and began to braid them.

On the third of April the storeboat stopped at a well-tilled clearing on the Ohio side. The fields were sheltered on every side by hills and deep forests and were enclosed by worm fences made of split rails laid zigzag.

The owner, a big ruddy gray-haired farmer, came down to the boat with a basket full of radishes, spring onions and fresh asparagus.

"I'm short of cash, storemaster," he said to Father, "but I'd like to make a trade with you."

"What do you need, friend?" asked Father.

"Four horseshoes and the nails to go with them."

"I'll take the vegetables in trade, if you'll throw in a basketful of greens for my cow," Father said.

"It's a bargain."

The farmer put two fingers in his mouth and gave a shrill whistle.

"That's to call my son," he said. "He's down at the pigsty. I've got my pigs shut up for fatting."

A tall young man vaulted over the fence at the far corner of the clearing and strode across the field to the boat.

"This is my son Simon—Simon Winthrop," said the farmer proudly.

Simon wiped his grimy hands on his brown homespun pantaloons and smiled shyly, with a gleam of white teeth. His clear gray eyes fastened upon Susan and widened a little.

"Simon," said his father, "get the sickle and cut a basketful of the grass in the far field. The storemaster wants some greens for his cow."

"All right, Dad," the young man replied, still looking at Susan.

"May I go with you and take our dogs?" asked Steve.

"And me too?" said David eagerly.

Simon nodded and turned to leave. The boys jumped off the boat and raced ahead, with Brownie and Patch frisking at their heels.

"Mother, may I go too?" Susan asked.

"Of course, child."

She hurried off the boat and fell into step beside Simon, trying to keep up with his long strides. He gave her a sidelong glance and reddened.

"Do you mind if I come with you?" she asked.

"Mind?" He gave a short embarrassed laugh. "I wanted to suggest it, but I didn't dare."

"Why not?"

"Well, I didn't think you'd be interested in my talk. By your dress and your speech, you're city folks."

"Oh, but I like farm folks best," Susan insisted. "They always seem so glad to see us."

"It's a rare treat to have somebody to talk to," said Simon simply. "And if it's no offense, miss, I don't reckon I ever saw anybody prettier than you are."

He stopped short and said hastily, "I've got to fetch the sickle and the basket. Don't go away."

He turned and ran toward the neat white farmhouse.

Steve and David circled the first field and came back, leaping from furrow to furrow between the rows of green growing grain. The two dogs had jumped the fence and were barking through the woods beyond.

"Isn't this an elegant farm?" Steve cried. "It's way ahead of any we've seen."

David was still puffing with the effort to keep up with his long-legged brother. The two boys waited with Susan until Simon trotted up, and they all walked slowly across the field. They arrived at a freshly harrowed stretch.

"I was fixing to plant the late onions when I finished feeding the pigs," Simon remarked. "See, there's my basket of onion sets."

"We're keeping you from your chores," Susan said apologetically.

"It's an honor, Miss—Miss—"

"Susan Doak," she told him.

"Miss Susan. That's a nice name."

Steve spoke up. "Dave and I will help you, if you'll show us how to plant the onions."

Simon showed them how to press a hole in the soft earth and set out the little brown onions in straight rows. Then he and Susan left them and went on to the grassy field at the edge of the farm.

She sat on the rail fence with her chin in the palm of one hand, and watched him cut the grass with short powerful strokes and scoop it into the basket.

He asked many questions. Where did they come from, why and when, what had they seen along the way, where were they going. When Susan mentioned Cincinnati, he straightened up with a brilliant smile.

"I'm going to Cincinnati after the harvest is in," he announced. "I'm going to read law with Judge Burnet."

"How can you bear to leave such an elegant farm?" she asked.

"Oh, I know I won't like being cooped up in an office all day," he said cheerfully. "But seems like I've just got to learn more."

Susan's brown eyes wandered to the field beyond the

white house, where four sleek horses were cropping the grass.

"Did you have to go far to school?" she asked.

"I never went to school," he said. "There's no school within twenty miles. Dad and Mother taught me my letters, and since then I've read everything I could lay my hands on."

Susan studied his clean-cut face, tanned by long days in the sun. He finally looked up and smiled.

"I reckon you think I'm foolhardy to want education so bad, when I've got so little."

"I don't at all," she contended warmly. "I was just thinking how easy it was for us to go to school in Pittsburgh, and how little we valued it."

"I reckon nobody values anything unless it comes hard," Simon said soberly.

He was wielding the sickle more slowly, but at length the basket would hold no more.

"Do you think that's enough?" he asked. "I could fetch another basket."

"One was all Father asked for," Susan said reluctantly.

They strolled back across the field, and the boys followed them to the storeboat. At a whistle from Steve, Brownie and Patch came crashing through the underbrush along the bank, splashed into the river up to their bellies, and began to lap at the water with long pink tongues. Then they climbed on board and shook themselves.

Susan drew Father aside and whispered to him.

"Father, Simon needs books terribly. Do give him a set of Franklin's works. Please, Father. I'll earn the money to pay for them somehow."

Father held her off and looked at her flushed face. "Well, well!" he said.

"Please, Father. Tell him it's a present, but don't say anything about me."

"That set costs quite a few, child."

"I know, Father. But please!"

He patted her shoulder and walked over to Simon. "Young man," he said, "come down below. I have some books that might interest you."

Simon's face lighted up and he followed Father down the steps into the store.

Father lifted the six thick volumes down from the shelf next the doorway, and put them into the boy's hands.

"See what you can make of them, young man."

"I wish I could buy them, sir, but I haven't any money to spare. I'm saving up to study law in Cincinnati."

"Oh, so that's it," said Father, smiling. "But I'm not asking for money. The books are a present."

"I couldn't accept such a present, sir."

"Nonsense!" said Father brusquely. "Take your books and the horseshoes and stop all this dillydallying."

"I—I don't know how to thank you enough, sir," Simon stammered. "But some day I'll find a way."

"Come to see us in Cincinnati."

"You may count upon that, sir," said Simon firmly.

"I rather thought I could."

When the storeboat pushed off, Mr. Winthrop waved and shouted good-by and then walked away. But Simon stood on the shore with his armload of books and watched as long as he could. Susan continued to wave until the boat went around the bend.

"Seems like a fine young fellow, that Simon," Pappy commented, with a glance at Susan's rosy face.

Steve began to chant mischievously:

> Simple Simon met a pieman
>   Going to the fair;
> Says Simple Simon to the pieman,
>   "Let me taste your ware."
>
> Says the pieman to Simple Simon,
>   "Show me first your penny";
> Says Simple Simon to the pieman,
>   "Indeed, I have not any."

David capered up and down the roof and around the rain barrels.

"Susie's getting mad!   Susie's getting mad!" he sang.

"Quit it, I say," Susan burst out, and ran down the hatchway.

Mother frowned. "For shame, boys. Susan's old enough to make friends with young men without being hectored by you two young rowdies."

"Oh, Mother, we didn't mean anything," Steve said. "I didn't even know I was teasing her until she began to squirm like an eel. She didn't have to get so uppish."

"All right. We won't talk about it any more." And Mother followed Susan downstairs.

She found the girl curled up on her pallet, crying into her pillow.

"Susie, dear, will you come and help me wash the asparagus and peel the potatoes?" Mother asked casually.

Susan raised her tear-stained face. "In a minute, Mother."

She dried her eyes on the hem of the calico sheet and joined her mother in the kitchen.

"Mother, why do they have to poke fun at Simon?"

"They weren't, dear," said Mother calmly. "They were laughing at you."

"But why?"

"You like Simon, don't you, Susan?" Mother asked abruptly.

"More than any boy I ever met. I can't explain it. He's —different."

"Well," said Mother, "I guess you're beginning to grow up. But don't pay any attention to the boys, because brothers always act like that."

"Mother, you liked Simon, didn't you?"

"Very much. Now get out the paring knife and tell me everything he said.'

Chapter XII

BUSINESS IN STEUBENVILLE

THE following day was Friday. Father turned over the steering to Pappy while he checked the account books with Susan.

"We'll probably be in Steubenville tonight," he said, as he ran his pencil down the long columns of figures. "I think it's about time I changed some of the silver dollars into gold eagles and half eagles, so we'll have more room in the money box."

Susan shook the box. "It's awfully heavy."

"Count the money while I finish adding," said Father. "I want to be sure the accounts and the money add up to the same figure."

Some time later, when they found that everything was in order, he said, "Now let's see about the goods we've taken in trade."

Susan reached over and turned to the back of the black ledger. "I've kept a list, Father, but I don't know if it's all right. It's so confusing when we buy part for ourselves and lay the rest aside for the store."

Father chewed his pencil and frowned over the list. At length he reached under the counter for the old slate and wrote down the extras that had to be sold.

"Two barrels of wheat flour, three flitches of bacon, two dozen raccoon skins, a barrel of salt and a barrel of maple sugar. Where in the name of green persimmons are we putting all this?"

Susan burst out laughing. "Why, in your cabin, Father."

"Oh! that explains the peculiar smell I mentioned to your mother last night. Well, it's time we got rid of them."

"There's something else, Father. I never wrote down Simon's books, because I mean to pay for them some way."

"Enter them as bought and paid for," said Father. "I'll put the money in the box out of my own pocket, and you can repay me later."

"Thank you, Father. When we get to Cincinnati I can hire out to some rich folks as a teacher or sewing woman."

"Don't worry about that, Susie," said Father. "I've been thinking I ought to pay wages to my whole crew. I can't pay you every week like Pappy, but I'll settle with you after I see Mr. Riddle. Your share ought to take care of the Franklin set."

Susan threw her arms around him. "Oh, Father, how elegant!"

"Oh, pish! I'm only looking after my own interests. I have to get those books paid for, don't I?"

Late that afternoon in a glorious sunset that spread over the entire sky, the storeboat lay by at Steubenville. The landing place was deserted and no one noticed their arrival.

"Davie, jump off and tie us to that big stake," said Father. "We can take our choice this evening, though by dawn we'll most likely have plenty of company. Saturday's a big market day."

Later at the supper table Mother said, "Let's have breakfast early tomorrow. I think the young folks ought to go to see the market. They might find something interesting."

Following her suggestion, Susan and the boys hurried through breakfast the next morning, and went ashore while the countryside was still tinged with the strange golden light of sunrise. A dozen skiffs had arrived during the night, and there was a subdued hum of activity along the riverfront.

The doors of the market house were open, and the stalls were piled high with big baskets of early green vegetables, slabs of fresh red meat, live fowls with their legs tied together, one and two pound pats of yellow butter embossed with the design of the farmer's butter mold, ground corn meal and wheat flour, potatoes and carrots.

While the three young Doaks stood in the entrance to the market house, watching the bustle within, they heard a halloo. A team of bays drew up in the cobbled street beside them. Sitting on the driver's seat of the wagon was Simon. His gray eyes were heavy with fatigue, but he grinned cheerfully.

"How come you to be here?" Susan asked in amazement.

"I drove all night," said Simon. "It's only thirty miles."

"Only thirty miles!" Steve exclaimed. "That's an awful lot. How long are you going to stay?"

"Till I trade away my load. I generally get home by nightfall."

Susan's face fell. "I wish you'd have dinner with us on the boat. I'm sure Mother would like to have you."

Simon shook his head. "That's mighty nice of you, but I can't stay long enough."

David pointed across the street. "Why, there's Father! What's he doing with a wheelbarrow?"

Father trundled the barrow across the street. "Hello,

Simon. I've been looking for you. Your father told me you'd be here today."

"Father!" Susan scolded. "Why didn't you tell us?"

"I thought you knew. I thought that was why you rushed off the boat before the breakfast dishes were cleared off."

"No, that was Mother's idea."

"Mrs. Doak told me to ask you to have dinner with us, Simon," said Father.

"Miss Susan asked me too, sir, but I expect to be on my way home by noon."

"That's too bad, Simon. Well, boys, let's not keep him from his business. Steve, take this wheelbarrow down to the landing and fetch a couple of those barrels up to Mr. Buttermore's store. He's going to buy all the goods we took in trade."

Susan lingered to watch Simon's horses while he went into the market house to bargain. After a short time he came out with two men who helped him unload the wagon and carry in the big baskets.

"I guess seeing you brought me good luck, Miss Susan," he said, as he handed down the last of the baskets. "I got a good price for my wares this morning, and that means a lot to me. Every dime carries me nearer Cincinnati."

Susan patted the nose of the mare nearest her. "I'm glad."

He jumped down from the wagon and strode into the market. He returned balancing a tall stack of empty baskets, which he heaved into the wagon. Then he turned and looked down at Susan.

"I hope you don't mind my saying so, Miss Susan, but I

declare you're even prettier than I remembered, with your eyes shining like that."

Susan blushed and dropped her eyes.

"Don't look away, Miss Susan," he begged.

She glanced down the cobbled street. "Oh, there come the boys with the wheelbarrow," she said inanely.

"I'll help them." And Simon dashed across the street. She saw him wave the boys aside and take the handles of the loaded barrow.

In a few moments he was back again. "I guess you're mad at me for saying such things," he said.

"No, I'm not," she insisted. "But now that you've sold everything, you can have dinner with us, can't you?"

"Really I can't, Miss Susan."

She stamped her foot. "You're saying that because you don't want to come."

For a moment a hurt look came into his eyes, and then he smiled. "I guess you don't understand how much I want to. There's a lot of things I want to do—and say."

"Then why don't you?" she burst out angrily.

He shook his head and smiled again. "Not until I get to Cincinnati," he said.

He sprang into the driver's seat and gathered the reins into his strong brown hands.

"Good-by, Miss Susan, until Cincinnati. Giddap!"

He chirruped to the horses and they swung the wagon around and clattered off. Twice he turned in the seat and waved. The second time Susan waved back.

The boys came out of Buttermore's Emporium with the wheelbarrow.

"Is Simon gone?" Steve called out.

Susan nodded and crossed the street. She walked back to the storeboat with them, keeping her eyes straight before her.

Ignoring her silence, Steve went on talking. "Isn't this a nice town? Pappy says there are twice as many stores as there are taverns. That's always a good sign. There's a paper factory here I'd like to see. They've got a steam engine, like the paper works in Pittsburgh. Don't you want to see it, Susan?"

"I might as well," she said.

Father and Pappy were waiting for the wheelbarrow at the landing. They had carried the rest of the barrels off the boat, and were counting the raccoon skins again.

"Let's try to pile the whole lot on the barrow this time," said Father. "Did you persuade Simon to change his mind about dinner, Susie?"

"No," she said miserably. "Can't you stop talking about it?"

Father blinked. "Well, in that case, we'll shove off as soon as we unload this stuff on Mr. Buttermore."

He and Pappy hoisted the two barrels into the wheelbarrow and jiggled it to see if they were steady. Then they piled the bacon and skins on top.

"Will we have time enough to go and see the steam paper mill, Father?" Steve asked anxiously.

"I'll take this load, George," offered Pappy. "Let the young folks run along and see the paper mill."

"Oh, thank you, Pappy! We'll do something nice for you some day," said Steve. "Come along, Dave. Hurry up, Susan, don't stand there looking so gloomy."

Susan almost had to run to keep up with Steve, and David

was panting. They passed the woolen factory, where they saw men and women sorting the fleece into large bins, while others scoured the wool, dipped it into great dye-vats, and carded it into strands. They heard the spinning and weaving machinery in another part of the building, but did not stop to investigate.

There was a flour mill, hazy with dust. One of the millers stepped to the door for a breath of fresh air as they hurried past. His hair, face and jacket were covered with the fine white powder.

At last they came to the paper factory. Looking through the windows, they saw the chugging steam engine which ran all the machinery, from the big vat where rags were ground into pulp to the round heated drums which pressed and dried the finished sheets of paper.

"Look at her!" said Steve, with eyes for nothing but the steam engine. "How she makes those wheels go round!"

But the others were more interested in what happened to the old cotton and linen rags in their transformation into writing paper.

"I wonder if Mother would give me some rags," David said. "I'd like to try that. I could use a flatiron to press the paper smooth."

"I don't want to discourage you," Susan said, "but I think they use some kind of chemical to make the pulp. Don't they, Steve?"

"I guess so," Steve agreed absently. "They keep that engine nice and shiny, don't they?"

A man passing through the engine room looked out and smiled at them, as they stood with their noses against the pane. He motioned to them to come in.

Once inside, Steve went straight to the steam engine, and walked around it.

"Like engines, young man?" the man said. "We've just had this one a few months. Before that we made every sheet by hand. Now with this machinery we could make two and a half tons of paper in twenty-four hours."

"That seems like a lot," Susan remarked.

Steve was still silently studying the machinery.

"Maybe you young folks would like a piece of paper to take home with you."

The man gave them each a sheet of white paper, still warm from the rollers. They thanked him politely and started back to the boat.

"We'll have to hurry," said Susan. "It must be late."

"Do you know what I'm going to do with my paper?" David puffed, skipping along beside the older two. "I'm going to draw a picture of a keelboat, with a passenger cabin, two masts, and a great big cargo box for the freight."

"I hope I won't forget how that engine worked," said Steve.

Dinner was ready when they climbed on board the boat.

"Are your hands clean, boys?" Mother said. "Hurry up and come to the table before everything gets cold. You can tell us what you saw while you're eating."

After dinner, while the sun was still directly overhead in the cloudless sky, the men and boys went up on the roof, leaving Mother and Susan to wash the dishes. The boat creaked, and some of the hot suds slopped out of the dish-pan as they pushed out from shore.

"Mother," Susan began, "Simon doesn't like us."

"What makes you think that, dear?"

"Because he could have stayed to dinner if he'd wanted to."

Mother held a plate up to the light to see if it was clean. "Maybe he had good reason," she said.

"But what could it be, Mother? Surely it doesn't matter so much if he's an hour or two late. His father wouldn't scold, and he's not afraid to travel after dark."

"Maybe he likes us too well to stay," said Mother.

"That sounds mighty silly to me, Mother."

"I have a notion Simon is too proud to want to be beholden to us for favors he can't repay. He's already indebted to us for the set of Franklin's works."

"Mother, I'll tell you something, if you'll promise never to tell Simon. It was I who gave him the books, not Father."

"There! We're all done except the pots. You can run along now. Yes, I know all about the books, but I'll let you tell Simon yourself some day."

"Mother."

"Yes, Susie?"

"I'm not so mad at Simon now. You—you make things seem better."

She skipped out of the kitchen and climbed up to the roof. The boys and Pappy were sitting with their feet hanging over, facing the Ohio shore, where a good dirt road wound along the bank. Susan sat down beside Pappy.

"What a lot of wagons there are on the road!" she said.

"We've counted eight going to Steubenville, and eleven big covered wagons going West," David announced.

"There's another!" cried Steve. "That makes twelve."

They saw a party of ten young men and women on horseback, the men carrying umbrellas over the heads of their partners to shade them from the sun.

"I wonder if they're going to a play-party," Susan said.

Pappy reached for Katy on the roof behind him, and began a cheerful tune.

"More likely they're just taking a walk on horseback," he said drily. "Seems like Americans don't care for shank's mare. Nobody walks a step if there's a critter handy, and there most generally is. I'll wager you'll have a critter apiece before the year's out."

"Oh, what fun we're going to have," Susan said gaily.

"Well," Steve observed, "I see you've perked up."

Chapter XIII

THE BOYS DECIDE TO WALK

ANOTHER day a tall sallow man hailed the storeboat near a log cabin in the midst of a deep Virginia forest. "Hello, the boat! Have you got a blade for a crosscut saw?"

Father and Pappy made a landing and looked curiously about them. The cabin was new and the windows were without panes. The settler had succeeded in clearing only a hundred feet or less of timber, and the stumps were still standing.

"But it's rich bottom land, once you get down to it," he said. "And there's plenty of game for anybody's rifle."

"Any turkeys around here?" Pappy asked. "I'd like to set my teeth in a juicy drumstick right now."

"Yes, there's turkeys. My brother shot two last week."

Steve and David looked at each other. "Father," Steve said, "we'd like to go ashore for a while. May I take my rifle and the dogs?"

"Them's pointer dogs," the settler remarked. "They make good hunters if you can keep them from yawping."

"May we go, Father?"

Father turned to the woodsman. "Any panthers in these parts?"

"Nary a painter this side of the hurricane tract up toward Chillicothe."

"All right, boys. Do you think you're going to find a turkey?"

"Maybe."

The settler shook his head doubtfully. "You mought, and again you moughtn't. The turkey is a right timorsome bird, and you have to have the knack of creeping up on him. My brother can, but I can't, though I hear them a-gobbling in the woods now and again."

"Well, a walk won't hurt you boys," said Father. "Keep near the river and head downstream, and we'll pick you up when you get tired."

The two boys started off cheerfully, with Steve's long heavy rifle, the small curved powder horn, and the square leather pouch containing his bullets, flint and tinder. At a stern word from the older boy, the dogs kept quietly to his heels.

They crossed the little clearing and plunged into the woods. The sunlight flickered through the branches overhead and cast patterns on the moss and dried leaves beneath.

David squinted up at the blue sky.

"Oh, my!" he said. "It makes me dizzy. I never saw such tall trees. What kind are they?"

"Oaks, elms, red maples, I guess. I'll wager it's dark in these woods when all the leaves are out."

A fat squirrel scampered out on a low branch and scolded angrily. Patch sprang forward with a deep growl.

"Quiet!" Steve ordered. The dog slunk back and whimpered.

"We don't want anything but turkeys, do we, Steve?"

"No, no little game for us."

They walked along in silence for some time, steering

around the giant trees that had fallen and taking care not
to step on any twigs that might crackle. Except for the
occasional song of a wood thrush or the chattering of squirrels, there was hardly a sound.

David glanced about him. "We're miles away from
everything," he said in a low tone. "Suppose we got lost!"

"I was thinking about that," said Steve. "Hush! Look
at Brownie and Patch!"

The dogs had halted and were standing motionless with
their tails in a straight line, noses pointed toward a scraggly
thicket off to the left.

"A turkey!" Steve whispered.

He deftly loaded the rifle and crept toward the thicket.
As he drew near, there was a noise like a snort. He raised
his gun, ready to strike the flint.

"It's a bear!" David said in a piercing whisper. "Let's
run!"

Steve shook his head and took another step. Then he
lowered the gun and began to laugh.

"Sooey!" he shouted.

A great sandy-colored hog tore out of the thicket and
scurried off, grunting and squealing. The dogs gave chase
with loud barks that rang through the forest.

Steve dropped his rifle and laughed until he rolled on the
ground among the brown leaves. David threw himself on
the ground and kicked up his heels.

"Turkeys! Bears!" said Steve, with a whoop. "Wait till
Pappy hears about this."

"And Father and Susan," David giggled, "and Mother."

Steve wiped his eyes on his blue calico sleeve and began
to laugh all over again. Finally he sat up.

"Well," he said, "if there ever was a turkey around here, I guess we scared him all the way to Tennessee."

The boys got up and brushed the leaves out of their hair and off their clothes.

"Here, Brownie! Here, Patch! Now maybe we've lost the dogs." Steve whistled and whistled.

After a minute he said, "Dave, you whistle a while. I'm all out of breath."

David took it up, and whistled until he was gasping for breath. At length the dogs loped into sight among the big tree trunks. They ran up wagging their tails and leaped at the boys, licking their faces until they cried out.

Steve pushed the dogs away and wiped his face. "Well, I hope the boat waits for us. Let's get a little piece on our way."

He picked up the rifle and the powder horn, and looked in his pouch.

"Tarnation!" he exclaimed. "The tinderbox must have fallen out of the pouch. Help me hunt, Dave."

They scuffed among the leaves, but the dogs made the search harder by digging until the leaves flew.

"Get out of the way, Brownie," David said. "You'll get your nose kicked. Oh, there it is, Steve!"

Both boys and dogs made a dive for the shiny tinderbox, and David rescued it from Patch's jaws before the dog could dash off with it.

"Now which way do we go, Steve?"

The older boy scratched his tousled red head. "I'm all turned around. This way, I guess."

They set off again. In every direction they could see nothing but trees, and there were no paths. A twig dropped on Steve's head. He looked up and saw a red squirrel scampering from branch to branch ahead of him.

"I don't like to kill him," he said, "but as long as we can't have turkey, fried squirrel is pretty good. I'm mighty tired of fish and salt meat."

He took painstaking aim, fired, and the squirrel dropped.

"Fetch it, Brownie!"

The dog brought him the squirrel, and he handed it to David, who swung it by the tail at his belt. Steve reloaded the gun carefully and they walked on.

Another squirrel and another fell as the crack of the rifle disturbed the quiet of the forest.

"Let me try, Steve," David begged.

He could hardly hold the long rifle steady, but he pointed it at the next squirrel, and fired. The kickback of the gun sent him sprawling.

"You hit him!" Steve said excitedly. "But he's still alive. Quick! We can't leave him like that."

He hastily cleaned and reloaded the rifle, and as his shot rang out, the squirrel fell. Brownie ran to fetch it.

David got up and dusted himself off. "I could have killed him right off if the gun hadn't hit back at me," he said.

Steve tossed the limp squirrel to him. "You'd better practice some more before you try shooting live critters, Dave," he said quietly. " 'Tain't fair to shoot just for the pleasure, and leave them to starve because they can't step lively any more."

David kicked at a moss-covered rock and hung his head.

"I'm getting awful tired," he mumbled. "Don't you think we've got enough for supper now?"

"I reckon so."

They quickened their pace and strode along without speaking. Finally David stopped and looked around again.

"Steve, there's nothing but trees anywhere," he faltered.

"Looks like it," Steve agreed. "Come on. We must make haste."

"Maybe we're lost!"

"I guess so. Pretty soon it will get dark. It gets dark sooner in the woods than it does on the river. And we'll be all alone in the dark with the wildcats and hoot-owls all around us."

"Steve! Quit it!"

Steve's eyes began to twinkle, but David did not notice.

"Maybe a panther swam across the river from Ohio, and is waiting on a limb up in that big oak tree yonder. We'll build a fire to keep warm, and that'll keep the wildcats and panthers and wolves away for a while. They'll sit around in a ring with their eyes shining at us. As soon as we go to sleep, the fire will go out, and they'll rush in and GRAB us!"

David turned a white face to him. "Does it really happen like that? Or are you trying to scare me?"

"Don't you think that would be exciting?"

"Steve, I wish you'd quit. Let's get out of here."

"Wait a minute." Steve walked around a tree, studying its gnarled trunk. "Here's the mossy side. That means this is north. Now the river ought to be somewhere to the northwest. Let's head straight for that patch of sunlight yonder and keep on in a straight line from there."

They broke into a jog trot and hurdled the logs that got in their way. David clutched at the squirrels fastened under his belt and began to puff. Brownie and Patch raced ahead, wheeled and came back, then ran off again. In a few moments they were out of sight.

At the sound of their distant barking, Steve shouted, "They've found the boat!"

They tore along until they began to sniff the faint odor of fish and decayed vegetation that indicated the river was near. Finally they emerged among the willows at the water's edge, but there was no storeboat. A neat little two-masted barge was disappearing around a bend with a flash of oars. They could still hear the patroon's voice crying, "Pull! pull! pull!"

A flatboat floated past. At one end was a haystack, around which five cows were feeding. In the doorway of the cabin, a woman in spectacles sat in a rocking chair and knitted. Her knitting needles flashed in the late afternoon sunlight. Two men and three boys were sitting at the stern, trailing fishlines in the wake of the craft.

Steve and David hallooed from the bank, and received an answering shout from the boys on board. Brownie and Patch made several threatening dashes into the water and barked frantically.

And still no storeboat. When the flatboat had passed, there was not even a leaf on the surface of the river. Two crows flew overhead, cawing raucously.

David swallowed hard. "What'll we do, Steve?"

Steve squared his shoulders. "We'll be all right. Don't worry. We've got the dogs and the rifle for protection. Besides, maybe the boat stopped on the Ohio side to sell something."

He began to whistle, but it was not a tune. Then he stopped and cocked his head.

"Listen!" he said, and a smile spread over his freckled face. "Isn't that Katy?"

More and more distinctly they heard the sound of a fiddle.

"There she comes round the bend!" cried David excitedly.

Steve cupped his hands. "Hello, the boat!"

"Hello, the mighty Nimrods!"

The boys waited impatiently to see Father and Pappy run the storeboat ashore at their feet. Instead, Father kept his course in the middle of the river.

"Father!" Steve wailed.

Father waved and grinned broadly. Pappy, sitting cross-legged on the roof, switched to a doleful tune. The storeboat nosed around the next bend, out of sight.

"I guess we walk," Steve said. "Come on."

He whistled to the dogs and they trudged along, keeping close to the bank. Sometimes they had to seize the willow branches to keep from slithering into the river.

"They can't go very far before we catch up with them," Steve said. "We can walk faster than they can float. The current's only two or three miles an hour. Pappy said so."

"We ought to have swum after the boat when it passed," David said.

"We may have to, at that." Steve grinned ruefully.

But when they swung around the sharp bend, the boat was waiting, made fast to a willow tree on the bank.

The rest of the family greeted them with loud cheers and a great blast on the horn. Warm and breathless, the boys climbed on board, and the dogs leaped to the deck beside them.

"Where's my turkey?" Pappy demanded. "Them ain't no turkeys dangling from Davie's belt."

Between giggles the boys told the story of the big sandy hog.

"So that," Steve concluded, "is why we thought we'd better take what we could find, which was squirrels. But after that trick you played on us, Dave and I are going to eat them all ourselves."

"Every scrap!" said David.

"I wonder who's going to cook them," said Mother, as if talking to herself.

"Well, you can have some, Mother," Steve conceded.

"That's good," said Mother. "But I always give your father part of my supper."

Father spoke up. "And I always share with Pappy."

"I always give everything away to the girls," Pappy drawled. "I wouldn't leave Miss Susie out."

"So I guess that fixes us all, doesn't it?" said Mother serenely.

"Why didn't you stop for us, Father?" Steve asked.

"I thought you wanted to walk," said Father in mild surprise. "Besides, there's a cabin over yonder. Your mother wants to see if she can buy a couple of loaves of bread. She says she can't bake bread in her bake-oven."

"Hello, the boat!" A tall gaunt man was thrusting his way through the bushes.

"Howdy, stranger," Father returned.

"Have you got any sugar aboard the boat?"

"Plenty. Will you step into the store?"

Down below, the man looked around and nodded approvingly. "That's a fine chance of dry goods, storemaster."

"The best. Can I make a bargain with you? I don't ordinarily sell groceries, but I think we can spare some sugar from our own barrel. And then you might buy some of our store goods. They're dog cheap, considering what you get for your money."

"That's a recommendation," said the farmer. "But I'd be mighty obliged if you'd just sell me some sugar. My old woman's making apple butter. Seems the rot's getting into the apples in my root-cellar, and she's run out of sugar trying to use them up."

Mother came down the little ladder. "Can you tell me what day your wife does her baking?" she asked.

"Wednesday, I reckon."

"Would she be able to spare two loaves of bread? How much do you think she'd take for them?"

The man pointed to the shelves. "For a piece of calico like that," he said, "I reckon she'd swap you the whole batch and eat corn pone for a week."

"It's a bargain," said Father. "Let's fetch the madam."

After long consultation with the farmer's plump wife, a trade was made, and the storeboat set off again, the richer by three loaves of fresh bread, a barrel of flour, a peck of dried apples, and a kettleful of apple butter.

"I hope she'll like those calicoes when she gets them made up," said Mother doubtfully. "They weren't what I'd pick for her. But she does make good bread."

Chapter XIV

MORE NEW FACES

FARTHER down the river, a day or two later, the storeboat floated to a landing near a little white frame house enclosed by a neat picket fence. The yard was a mass of pink and white phlox. At the rear were a small barn and a log cabin.

The blast of the horn brought a pleasant Negro man down to the shore to present his mistress' compliments and invite the visitors to come and sit a while with her during the heat of the day.

So Mother and Susan went to call upon the Widow Clarke. They found her a plump rosy old woman, puffing on a clay pipe while she mended a tear in a Star of Bethlehem patchwork quilt.

"It's a rare honor for me to have company," she said. "With nobody to talk to except black Jake there, I sometimes get overcome with lone."

"You live here all alone?" Mother asked.

"Ever since Mr. Clarke died three years ago. But last summer I picked up and went to Philadelphia, where I come from."

"On the packet and the stagecoach?"

"Lands, no," said the old woman, with a puff on her pipe. "I just had Jake saddle my horse with one blanket under the saddle and one on top, and packed my saddlebags with vittles and clothes, and set out. Of course I took a heavy cloak and an umbrella in case of rain."

"And you went all that way by yourself?"

"'Twas only about seven hundred miles. Lands, I saw a woman in Harrisburg who'd traveled all the way from Tennessee on horseback with three babies!"

"I still think you were very brave," said Mother. "Don't you, Susan?"

The girl nodded, wide-eyed. "That's what you mean by not being too ladylike, isn't it, Mother?"

Mother laughed. "Yes, I reckon it is."

"'Tain't nothing to boast of," said the Widow Clarke. "I always was a tomboy. Tell me, does the storemaster know anything about cows?"

"I don't know," said Mother. "Is your cow sick?"

"She's got the tremblings and the staggers." The old woman raised her voice and called Jake.

The Negro came to the door. "Yes'm?"

"Where's Lissie, Jake?"

"Her bell's tinkling down by the berry patch, Miss Prue. I reckon she ain't gone far."

"Bring her in, but don't run her."

"No'm, Miss Prue, she ain't able to run."

"Susan," said Mother, "go and fetch your father. Maybe he'll know what's the matter."

Father came on shore and looked over the thin black and white cow that Jake led up to the picket fence.

"She looks mighty feeble," he said. "What do you feed her?"

"She feeds in the woods," the Widow Clarke replied.

"I'd try keeping her in for a while, and feed her on hay, Swedish turnips and wheat bran."

"Jake and I were sick last week from drinking her milk."

"She's probably feeding on weeds," said Father. "It can't hurt her to be shut up for a while. Might put some flesh on those bones."

The old woman thanked him and said, "Seems like I ought to pay you for your advice, same's I would a horse-doctor."

Father made a bow. "Madam, I never take money for advice, even when it's good."

"But I'd rather pay you. I have money enough."

"Well, I have plenty of advice," said Father, with a smile. "So we're even. I have as good a right to give you advice as you have to give me money."

After they left the Widow Clarke's, they made a number of stops before nightfall. Once in the middle of the afternoon, the dogs began to run up and down the deck, barking violently. David spotted a big white cat sunning himself on a little ledge in the steep bank. The cat yawned and stretched and coolly washed his face.

"Blow the horn, Davie," Father suggested. "Where there's cats, there's people."

At the first toot, four bearded young men brushed through the undergrowth and shouted frantically, as if afraid the boat might not stop. When they came on board they explained that another brother was building a new cabin in the woods for his bride. They needed all manner of hardware and house furnishings for the new home.

They laughed often and shoved each other as they tried to decide what to buy first. One brother, who seemed quieter than the others, bought nails, hinges, latches, screws,

and such. Another bought pots and pans and woodenware. The third chose a complete set of white crockery, and the fourth picked out some pewter tableware, brass candlesticks and a Bible.

The coins rattled into the money box faster than Susan could write in the account book, and Steve was kept busy making change. Finally the four men filed off the boat, each with a clanking gunny sack thrown over his shoulder, and went hallooing through the woods.

That night at sunset the storeboat was lashed to a stake beside a number of empty rafts at Charlestown, Virginia, a thriving town at the foot of the hills. As usual after supper, Pappy tuned up his fiddle for a little music before bedtime. But as he tightened the last string, there was a snap.

"Tarnation!" he said. "Busted a string."

The young people wailed.

"Is Katy broken for good?" David asked anxiously.

"No," said Pappy, "but now I got to find me a raccoon."

"What for?" David asked.

"Well, they speak of fiddle strings as catguts, but the insides of raccoons is more handy."

"I'll shoot a raccoon for you, Pappy," Steve offered. "I'll get off the boat as soon as it's dark and go through the woods with a flare. I'll wager Patch and Brownie can tree a raccoon for me."

"I ain't forgot the turkey you shot for me, Red," Pappy said, "but you know raccoons is harder to find than turkeys."

Steve reddened through his freckles, but he laughed. "I can try."

"Howsomever," said Pappy, "it'd be easier to find a boy

who lives around here and knows where to look for raccoons."

The next morning while the sky was still gray above the hills, Steve and Pappy went ashore to look for a boy.

"While we're here, Steve, there's something I want to show you," said Pappy. "Look over there in front of the courthouse."

Steve stared at a large wooden framework with three holes in it. "What is it? An old-fashioned pillory?"

"That's right. Ain't it a shame and a disgrace, in a free country?"

Steve ran over and put his head and hands through the openings, and sat down on the sharp iron bar behind him.

"Oh, Pappy, it would be awful if you had to stay here long."

"Yes, you'd be locked in there, with folks staring at you."

"It gives me the mulligrubs," said Steve, climbing out.

"I got no doubts it gave plenty of folks the mulligrubs in its time," Pappy said.

"Do they still use it to punish folks?"

"I've heard so, Red, but I never seen it in use. You'd think the town would tear it down and make a bonfire of it."

A sturdy boy in brown homespun came whistling down the street. Pappy hailed him.

"Know where I can find a raccoon, son?"

"Live or dead?" The boy eyed them suspiciously.

"It don't matter," Pappy said.

"I got a dead one in my backyard," the boy said. "But I ain't skinned him yet. The skin costs a quarter."

"I don't want the skin, son, but I'll give you five cents for the carcass."

"What do you want it for?"

"Fiddle strings. Now don't ax no more questions, but fetch me that carcass as quick as you can. I'll be waiting on the storeboat down at the landing."

The boy turned and trudged up the dusty street. On the way back to the boat Pappy pointed out four warehouses.

"They're full of flour for the New Orleans trade. Them rafts down on the river is waiting for cargoes."

Within half an hour the boy appeared with the skinned raccoon, and by the time the boat shoved off, Pappy had stretched the new fiddle strings to dry between two nails on the outside cabin wall.

The whole family missed the music, and Pappy hardly knew what to do with himself without Katy. For two days, however, Mother and Susan were almost too busy to notice the lack. The washing, which had been postponed so long, had to be done.

The boys dipped bucketfuls of rain water from the barrels on the roof and filled the kettles on the stove. The soiled clothes were put to soak in tubs of hot suds on the kitchen floor. As Mother or Susan finished scrubbing, they tossed them into a large basket.

When the basket was full the boys carried it up to the roof and dumped the contents into the first tubful of rinsing water.

At length everything was wrung out and hung on the clotheslines which Father set up on the roof. High-waisted calico and gingham dresses, heavy petticoats, frilled shirts, plain shirts with hardly a ruffle, pantaloons, and yards of household linens flapped in the wind.

"Fiddlesticks!" Father grumbled, peering over the clothes-lines as he steered. "Where did we ever get so much frippery? I can't see where we're going."

"It will be over in a few hours," Mother said calmly, removing a clothes-peg from her mouth. "There's a good dry breeze."

"I'll man the oar, George," Pappy offered. "You post yourself at the bows as lookout man if you want to, but I can navigate this river blindfolded."

With a grin Father turned over the steering oar to Pappy and crawled under the clotheslines to the front of the boat.

"Channel swerves right, Pappy," he called out. "Good! Now straighten her."

After a few minutes of this, Pappy said, "You don't see a farmhouse, do you, George? Seems like there ought to be one along here."

"Not finding it hard to steer, are you, Pappy?" Father was chuckling.

"No, George," the old man drawled. "I was just worrying about the state of the money box."

"Don't you worry about that money box. Whoops! heave her to the left! There's a sawyer!"

The storeboat grazed the branches of a submerged tree, but kept her course.

"Next time something like that happens, George, send me a letter ahead of time, so's I won't be so scared."

"Hurray! There's a cabin on the Ohio side. David, where's your horn?"

David, fishing at the stern, jumped up and ran along the deck, tripping over the dogs.

"It's on the roof somewhere, Father. Can you hand it to me?"

Father found the horn, and the boy blew a long blast.

"The coast is clear ahead and on the shore, Pappy. Heave her to," Father directed.

"I can see the shore," Pappy replied. "It's the middle of the stream I was worried about."

Steve and Father helped with the sweeps, and the boat nosed gently into the bank.

Their customer this time was a fair-haired, rosy-cheeked young woman about Susan's age, dressed in a short straight homespun dress. She wanted to buy only a new frying pan, but she could not take her eyes off the flower-trimmed leghorn bonnet on the shelf beside the Yankee notions.

"Oh, I'd admire to have a poke bonnet like that!" she breathed. "But my Pappy'd never allow it. He's a powerful religious man."

"That's the bonnet I want too," said Susan, "so I'm making one for myself. Would you like to see it?"

She brought out the braided grass bonnet which she had started.

"I have to gather more grasses," she said. "See, I splice them so there won't be any lumps, and then I sew the braid round and round. When it's finished it will be a poke like that one. It will tie under the chin with blue ribbons."

The farmer's girl looked at it carefully. "I know where I can get grass like that. Maybe if it didn't cost anything, Pappy wouldn't be so mad."

"Maybe your mother can persuade him," Susan suggested.

"I haven't any mother," the girl said. "I keep house for

my Pappy and the younger children. Lawsy, when my mother was alive, he'd have bought me that beautiful bonnet. He didn't get religion till after she died."

Father decided to wait until the washing was dry before going any farther, so the two girls went ashore with a basket to gather grasses.

As they walked through the woods swinging the basket, the farmer's girl told Susan that her name was Nancy and that she was the oldest of five children.

"I hope Pappy doesn't catch me running away from my chores," she said cheerfully. "Lots of times I run off to the woods while he's busy in the field, and sometimes he gives me a licking for it."

Susan looked shocked. "At your age!"

"Oh, but he's a very good man, I guess. He's just stern," Nancy said. "Well, here's the patch of grass. Is it long enough for you?"

"It's the best yet," said Susan enthusiastically.

They plucked until the basket was almost full.

"Look!" said Nancy. "Over yonder there's spice bush, and the violets and spring beauties are already in bloom."

"Let's pick some!" Susan cried.

"I'll help you pick," said Nancy. "But look out for poison ivy this time of year."

Chattering gaily, they strolled through the woods, picking flowers as they went, until Susan had her hands full.

"We'd better go back for the basket, I guess," she said.

Nancy glanced up at the sun through the trees as they started back.

"I'll have to start supper soon," she said reluctantly. "But it's been such fun."

"I'd better go home with you," said Susan. "If your father says anything, I'll tell him it was all my fault. It was, too."

"He won't be there yet," Nancy said.

"Well, let's divide up the grass so you can commence your bonnet."

Nancy shook her yellow head. "I can get plenty more. You take it all."

When they got back to the storeboat, Mother was on the roof taking down the last of the washing, and Father was rolling up the clotheslines.

"All aboard!" Father said. "The dogs had a romp on shore while you were gone and now they're ready to leave."

With a toot of the horn and repeated good-bys, they were off again, while Nancy watched them leave with wistful eyes.

The next day was ironing day. David kept the dogs on deck, away from the clean clothes. All day Susan stoked the fire in the kitchen stove to heat the flatirons, and she and Mother took turns at the ironing board. Now and then the boat jarred against the bank, and Father called Susan into the store to make the entries in the account books.

The stove threw out so much heat that they had to open both windows in the kitchen to admit the cool breeze, and the scent of the woods blended with the warm sweet smell of the hot iron on the sun-dried fabrics.

"Listen to the birds singing!" said Susan.

"Yes, spring is here for sure." Mother stepped over to the stove to change irons.

Susan buried her nose in the bowlful of violets and spring

beauties on the table. "They're so pretty. It's a pity they haven't any smell."

The noise of a loud drumming suddenly filled the kitchen.

"What on earth is that?" said Mother. "Have the boys been feeding the chickens and geese again?"

"It's much louder than usual," said Susan. "Sounds as if they're pecking on the wall."

She opened the little door into the pen and looked out. There was a whir of wings that flashed red and black in the sunlight, and the noise stopped.

"What was that?" asked Pappy from the roof.

"A woodpecker, I guess."

She closed the door and sat down again.

"I wish we could have that door open without being overrun with fowls," Mother said. "I wouldn't want to spend the whole summer on the boat without more air and an awning on the roof to keep out the heat."

Susan walked over and took the iron out of Mother's hand. "It's your turn to cool off, Mother," she said. She finished ironing the collar of a shirt. "Do you know, Mother, I don't know how we'll ever settle down in Cincinnati. You never know what's going to happen next on the river."

"I know," said Mother, fanning herself with her apron. "I reckon that's its fascination for your father and Pappy."

Gradually the pile of roughdried clothes diminished, and the stacks of smoothly ironed garments and linens grew higher. At last they were able to set away the flatirons to cool, and the hardest day of the week was over.

"Thank heaven!" Father said. "It'll take the rest of the week to get the smoke out of my eyes."

"Now, George," said Mother, "you know it wasn t as bad as that."

"Well, it might have been, if the wind hadn't blown the smoke away."

Chapter XV

INDIAN MOUNDS AND A SWORD

AS the days passed, town after town ceased to be mere names on the map, and became a reality that the young people were to remember vividly all their lives.

Toward the middle of April, there was Wheeling, built in a glen between bold hills. For some minutes before they reached the town, they heard the sound of hammering echo through the hills. Half the waterfront seemed to be given over to shipyards.

"There ain't no place to land, George," Pappy said, eyeing every keelboatman they passed. He greeted some with a roar and offered to take them on in a rough-and-tumble. Others he ignored.

Just ahead, a Kentucky broadhorn eased out into the river, leaving a space barely large enough for the storeboat. Father steered for the opening, and Steve made the boat fast to one of a row of heavy stakes driven into the gravel bank.

Susan and David sat on the edge of the roof to watch several men trying to coax three horses onto a raft tied near by. The horses strained at their halters and rolled their eyes in terror of the big red wagon which had already been rolled on board.

Father strolled off toward the United States bank to exchange a hundred and fifty heavy silver dollars for fifteen gold eagles, while Steve disappeared in the direction of the shipyards.

"Maybe a little of Katy's music would help those horses," Pappy remarked. "I'm going to see if my new fiddle string is ready for use."

He jumped down to the deck below and in a few minutes he had replaced the broken string. He vaulted back to the roof and began to play an old ballad air.

"Besides," he added, "if my friend Wilkins is anywheres around, he'll hear Katy and come a-raring up to finish that fight—maybe."

But no Wilkins appeared. After a while the horses calmed down and stamped aboard the raft. One of the men wiped his face with a blue bandanna handkerchief and smiled up at Pappy.

"That's elegant music, stranger," he said. "Ain't heard anything like that since we left Hagerstown."

"Going far?" asked Pappy.

"Indiana. We came across the mountains on the new National Road in good time, but we've got a long journey overland at the other end."

"You're right smart to take your critters with you," said Pappy. "They come dear in the West."

"So they say. Critters are plenty cheap here. Folks come overland from the South and sell everything to buy a boat. Seems like they can't build them fast enough. There was twenty folks a-sleeping on the floor of one tavern last night, and every bed full. More's coming in every day, too."

David looked up.

"Wouldn't it be fun," he said, "if everybody moved out of the East, and there was nothing left but empty houses?"

One of the other raftsmen interrupted. "Reckon we can pull out now."

With much neighing from the restive horses, the raft pushed out from shore and floated down the broad river.

Steve returned, whistling cheerfully. "I saw where the 'Washington' was built," he said, "and talked to a man that worked for Captain Shreve."

"Do pray tell," said Pappy. "Why, Red, maybe you even set foot on the very ground where Henry Shreve planted his heels. Looks to me like you're making a hero out of that man."

"Maybe I am," Steve confessed. "But I think what he's doing is just as important as leading an army."

In a few minutes Father strode down the steep bank, frowning.

"Let's get started," he said. "I'm as mad as a skinned wildcat in a beehive."

"What's the matter, George?"

"Why in the name of tin-tailed buzzards did you let me sell my flour in Steubenville? It's selling for five dollars a barrel here. Let's shove off."

The next few days were so profitable, however, that Father forgot his loss and recklessly proposed that they buy Sunday dinner on shore at Tomlinson's Ferry.

"I reckon you'd enjoy somebody else's cooking for a change, Miss Biddy," he said.

"I would, at that," she agreed.

"Anyway, I want the children to see the Indian mounds."

On Sunday morning they landed beside Mr. Tomlinson's ferryboat and went on shore. There was no one in sight, but a beaten path led them about half a mile through the scraggly woods to the big house. The dogs raced to the house first and touched noses with a big red setter lying under the porch steps.

A white-haired man came out and stood waiting on the porch.

"Hello, Tomlinson," Father called out. "Have you got enough dinner for six more?"

"Well, if it isn't George Doak! The old lady will be pleased."

Mrs. Tomlinson came to the door, wiping her hands on her pink gingham apron, and gave them a hearty welcome.

"What good smells!" said Mother, sniffing.

"Lucky I've got a beef roast in the oven," said Mrs. Tomlinson. "But if it ain't enough, I'll fry some chickens. Make yourselves at home, folks." And she returned to the kitchen.

Pappy squinted out across the green fields. "Where's them elk you had, Mr. Tomlinson?"

"They trampled down my fence and got away a couple of years ago. But one of them dropped an antler over three feet long. I've got it hanging on the wall for a hat-rack."

The boys and Susan went inside to look at the antler and tried to imagine the size of the animal that grew it.

"If I was in the woods and I met an elk like that," said David, "I'd lift my gun and go BANG!"

"And if I was the elk," said Steve, "I'd grin at you and walk away."

"No, you'd drop dead."

"I'll wager I wouldn't."

"Well, anyway, I'll be a good shot some day." David stalked out on the porch.

The grown people were sitting in a row of rocking chairs on the edge of the porch.

"I've been determined to get a printing press for five years," the ferryman was saying. "I figure I could print pamphlets or even a weekly newspaper. First thing I'd like to do is to get the old-timers to write up the early days before they all die off."

"Could you sell enough to make it pay?" asked Father.

"Might. There's a powerful lot of traffic on the river these days, and a shortage of reading matter."

David shook his sandy head. "I can't understand why folks hanker after book learning."

"You would, lad, if you didn't have none," said Pappy seriously. "I wouldn't be a rover if I'd had school learning. It gets wearisome, having nothing but mother wit and Katy."

"You're pretty well fixed at that, Pappy," said Mother, with a smile.

"Let's have a tune before dinner, Pappy," suggested Mr. Tomlinson. "A good tune's worth a wagonload of books."

After dinner, while Mother sat on the porch with Mrs. Tomlinson, the ferryman led the others out across the fields dotted with small mounds. He pointed to a much larger mound, nearly a hundred feet high, its summit overgrown with tall trees.

"That's where we're going," he said. "That's the Big Grave."

"Is that an Indian mound?" Steve asked in surprise. "It looks as big as a mountain."

"Folks used to think it was a mountain," said Mr. Tomlinson.

David left the path and began to climb the hardest way. Halfway up, he let out a whoop. "Look what I found! An arrowhead!"

"We used to find lots of those," said their host. "White ones, black ones, and pink ones. I've got a boxful of Indian relics back at the house."

David brought the white arrowhead for him to see. "I guess you need this one too," he said reluctantly.

"No, young fellow. You keep it."

David thanked him, and after wiping the piece of flint carefully on the seat of his calico pantaloons, put it in his pocket.

They reached the summit. Mr. Tomlinson picked up a heavy stick and beat on the ground.

"Do you hear that?" he said. "It's hollow. That's proof that it's an Indian burying-ground."

"What's in it?" Steve asked. "Just skeletons?"

"Well, I guess there's probably all the trappings an Indian would need in the happy hunting grounds in the hereafter."

"You've never tried digging, have you?" asked Father.

"No. I figure we'd better wait till the government can do it proper. It's one of the oldest mounds ever found."

"How can you tell that?" Steve asked. "Oh, I know. By the size of the trees growing here on top."

Glancing up at the immense branches that arched against the deep blue sky over their heads, Pappy said, "Seems to me these here trees is about as fine a monument as any man could wish."

By the time they returned to the house, two men and a woman were waiting for Mr. Tomlinson to ferry them across to Virginia, wagon and horses and all. The Doaks walked down to the landing by way of the short cut through the woods, and the storeboat was well out in the middle of the stream before the ferry was ready to shove off.

Within the next few days, they found themselves in more and more prosperous country. There were frequent stops at neat farmhouses surrounded by orchards in full flower and fields of growing wheat, rye, and sometimes flax and hemp. Often there were large pastures of grass and white clover for the sleek cattle.

On the eighteenth of April they came to the Long Reach, where the Ohio straightened out into a deep swift channel broken only by small islands covered with drooping willows.

"Don't you wish there weren't so many islands?" said David, leaving his fishline to look at the view ahead. "Wouldn't it be fun to see boats seventeen miles away?"

"You couldn't see anything as far away as that, Davie," Pappy said, "but I'll tell you something about that littlest island. Back in 1787 I hid an old Spanish sword in the sand there. Picked it up down river and didn't know what to do with it, so I hid it."

"Why didn't you carry it, Pappy?" David asked.

"Me carry a sword?" Pappy cackled. "In them days a tomahawk was more to the point."

"Is it still there?"

"Don't know. Never felt the need of a sword, so I never looked."

David's eyes shone. "Let's look now!"

Father studied the sandy shore of the little island. "I'm afraid we can't land there. That big willow hangs too low over the water."

"We could take the canoe," Steve suggested.

Pappy and the two boys lowered the canoe into the water and dropped into it. With both Steve and Pappy paddling, it took only a minute or two to reach the island and beach the canoe under the spreading boughs of the willow tree.

Old Pappy looked around and scratched his head. "The place has changed considerable," he said. "Seems to me there was nothing but sand and a lot of little willow trees."

"I guess one of the willows grew up and crowded the rest out," Steve remarked.

"Well, well, time does fly," said Pappy. "I reckon I did dig my hole on the downstream side of the biggest one of the lot. Pitch in, boys."

While David pulled weeds, Steve and Pappy scraped away the dead leaves and heaved aside several large mossy rocks. The old man picked up a stout stick and dug into the dark sandy earth.

"Struck something hard," he said. "Maybe just another rock."

He continued to poke, and soon uncovered a bit of red rust.

"Here she is!" he said in astonishment.

All three puffed and dug with their hands, and in a few minutes Pappy grasped the old sword in his hand, corroded with rust and caked with mold.

"It's yours if you want it, Davie."

David looked at it. "Oh!" he said. "I thought it would be shiny."

"That's just dirt and rust," said Steve. "You can scrape it off."

"The handle's silver," said Pappy. "All it needs is some soap and ashes."

David brightened. "And I can sharpen it with a whetstone until I can kill bears with it."

He took the long sword and tried to swing it in the air.

"Well, boys," said Pappy, "let's get back to the boat. Your paw can't even land her without some help from us."

As they paddled after the storeboat, they heard a dog baying in the woods. The sound came nearer. There was a rustle in the weeds on the high bank, and a rabbit leaped into the water and swam for the opposite shore. The dog crashed through the underbrush, paused to bark after the rabbit, then turned and disappeared into the tangle of vines and bushes.

The startled rabbit made a straight course across the river, passing within a few inches of the stern of the canoe. Pappy held his paddle out of the water while the little animal swam by.

"Why didn't you reach out and grab him, Pappy?" David asked.

"Well, I was afraid he'd kick me," Pappy drawled. "Spunky little fellow."

"I'm glad he got away," Steve confessed.

David held the sword over the side of the canoe and let the current wash off some of the dirt. When they caught up with the storeboat he clambered aboard calling for rags and soap.

"Quick!" he said. "You can see it later. I have to clean it."

Mother made him do his cleaning on the rear deck, where the litter he would make could be easily scrubbed away.

After a few days of steady rubbing and scraping, with help from Pappy, David had the chased silver handle shining and the blade almost clean. He stopped working on the sword just in time to brandish it threateningly at a keelboat making its way upstream. The boatmen were hauling the keelboat along by grabbing bushes and rocks on the steep banks.

"Hello, the boat!" roared the boatmen.

"Hello, the bushwhackers!" Father returned. "What's the news down river?"

"Nothing much. We pretty near got hit by a cannon ball at Cincinnati. They was firing salutes to General Harrison because he got back safe from the wars in the House of Congress."

"Did you meet the 'Washington' down below?"

"Two days from the Falls she was still afloat."

It was late in April and the locust trees were beginning to perfume the air when they reached Marietta, at the mouth of the Great Muskingum river in Ohio. Here too the shipyards were busy.

"Lot of seagoing schooners built here," Pappy remarked. "Going to run ashore, George?"

"I reckon not. There's nothing for us in Marietta. Too many stores. I'd rather stop at the settlement beyond, on the other bank of the Great Muskingum, where there's no store."

Steve looked glum. "I'd like to see those shipyards."

Now they were passing the wide mouth of the Muskingum. "I see they've got a ferry," he added. "What difference does it make where you stop? Folks can take the ferry across to Marietta to buy from us. There it goes now."

"Sorry, Red," said Father, steering for the shore. "We're stopping at the settlement."

"Did you ever see a ferry like that?" Pappy put in. "Run by the force of the current. The boat's tied to a traveling pulley that runs along that there rope swung across the river."

Steve and David stared.

"I don't see how the current could make it go across instead of downstream," Steve said. "But you're right. There's not a sign of an oar and the ferryman isn't using his pole. But he steers at a mighty funny angle."

"Wait till she starts back, Red," said Father. "You'll see why."

Steve stood on the low roof with his eyes glued on the ferryboat, while David blew the horn, and customers came and went across the deck just below him. He could hear Pappy fiddling away down in the store, and now and then Father's hearty laugh. Occasionally there was a clink of coins.

The ferryboat reached the shore at Marietta, discharged its passengers, and waited a long time before making the return trip. At last Steve saw the ferryman stand up and shove off with his pole, then take the tiller to steer. The boat swung around so that the upstream end was pointed toward the opposite shore, and it moved slowly across. Steve began to grin.

Father called up through the hatchway, "Found out yet how the ferry runs, Red?"

"Yes, Father. It depends on how the ferryboat is turned. It's the same principle as sailing, only he turns the boat instead of a sail."

"Right! Good boy, Steve!"

As the spring advanced, the days were lengthening and the nights were warmer. One dark night not far below Marietta, everyone on the storeboat was wakened by voices on the river. They were used to whippoorwills, hoot-owls, and even the howling of wolves at night. And often after the moon came up flatboats and keelboats passed, steering by the light of the moon. But the sound of voices and the dipping of a paddle was so unusual that it brought everyone but Pappy from their beds to the kitchen windows.

They discovered a canoe off the stern of the storeboat. There was a splash, as of an anchor dropped overboard. A boy in the prow held a flaming pine torch, while two men searched the water and speared fish with barbed gigs.

The Doaks shivered in their night clothes and watched the men land three large fish. Then Mother said she was cold, and went back to her warm bed.

David tried to rub the sleep out of his eyes. "Father," he said, "may I get dressed and go fishing with those folks?"

Father rumpled his hair. "You go back to bed before you catch your death, Bub. You'd be asleep before a fish could flip his tail. Come, let's all get some sleep."

"I'm not sleepy now," Steve protested. "I'd like to watch them a while."

"All right, but get your coat."

Steve wrapped himself in his coat and sat down by the window. It was a clear still night, and the torch cast a flickering path on the water. Once one of the men hurled his gig at something that flashed in the water and drew it back empty. The others laughed. But usually they did not miss.

After an hour or more, they strung their fish on a cord and hung it over the side of the canoe. Taking up their paddles, they guided the canoe to the shore, where they built a fire and made beds of small green branches.

The next morning at dawn the fishermen boarded the storeboat and offered to sell their fish for twenty-five cents apiece. They were all catfish weighing thirty pounds or more.

Mother shook her head. "I'm afraid they'd spoil before we could use them," she said. "Besides, our son keeps us well supplied with fish."

The men shrugged. "Well, we can sell them readily enough at Parkersburg," said one of them.

"You're more hopeful than I am about that village," said Father, with a laugh. "I figured I'd save myself the trouble of stopping there."

Chapter XVI

BLENNERHASSETT'S ISLAND

O N the last Monday in April Father made three different stops at Belpré, the settlement that stretched along the Ohio shore for five miles. Very few of the farmers could visit the village stores often, and the storeboat was welcomed.

At the first stop, Mother came into the store and said, "George, the rain barrels are empty. Ask some of the folks if they can spare some well water."

Father groaned. "It can't be washing day again."

"I've put it off too long as it is," said Mother.

She went back into the kitchen and began to sort out the soiled clothes according to color. Later she felt the boat move. They were pushing off from shore.

She called out through the open window, "Steve, you can start bringing down the water for the washing."

His voice floated down to her. "We haven't any water."

Mother looked grim and went to the hatchway. "George Doak, you forgot that water."

"Yes, ma'am," said Father cheerfully.

"Well, don't forget it next time."

The same thing happened at the second stop, and the third. Then Mother climbed up to the roof and glared at Father, unmindful of the wide grins of the children.

"George Doak, you're the most exasperating man I ever

knew," she said. "I have a sneaking notion you're doing this deliberately, because you don't enjoy washing day."

"Hell's a-snorting, George," Pappy murmured.

"Hold on, Miss Biddy," said Father, wagging a finger at her. "Temper, temper!"

Mother snorted. "The children haven't a clean rag to their names."

Father smiled fondly at her. "My, what beautiful eyes you have, Miss Biddy. I reckon you're too busy to notice that we're running ashore right now."

Mother looked. They were approaching the foot of a large island.

"George," she said, smiling in spite of herself, "you're a ninnyhammer. What island is this?"

"Did you ever hear of Blennerhassett's Island?"

"The same Blennerhassett who was accused of conspiracy with Aaron Burr?"

Susan spoke up. "Pappy has been telling us all about him. He was a rich Irishman who came to America about twenty years ago with his pretty bride. He spent nearly all his money on a fine house, and gave the rest to Aaron Burr to set up a new kingdom in the far Southwest. They thought they could all get rich there. But they were found out."

"That's just about the story," said Father. "Well, there's nothing much left of the house, but there's a good well. I thought we could build a fire and do the washing under the trees."

After a hasty dinner they went on shore, each carrying a tub or an armload of clothes.

"I reckon this is the very spot where Aaron Burr unloaded

his firearms," Father remarked. "He used the island as a gathering place for his militia."

"You could see campfires a-burning all over the island," said Pappy.

Father nodded. "I reckon we've seen a lot happen on this old river. Well, the rest of you'd better wait here while I find the well."

He set off across what had once been a smooth lawn, but was now a grassy clearing spotted with dandelions and weeds. Brownie and Patch followed him, wagging their tails.

The others set down their loads inside the great stone gateway, and gazed at the blackened ruins of the long curving colonnade facing them.

"Twenty years ago," Pappy said, "that was the finest house in the country, pretty near. Blennerhassett had a big library room and a scientific laboratory at one end and servants' quarters at the other, with the big house between. Now look at it."

"Did you ever visit the Blennerhassetts?" Mother asked.

"I ain't gentry," he replied shortly. "They didn't have much truck with common folks. Mrs. Blennerhassett was a good lady, according to her lights. She was good to the poor. When she had her own children vaccinated against the smallpox, she had the same done for all the poor children up and down river. But it was like she was royalty handing out favors. They both had an overdose of gentry."

"I've heard they had a fine art collection," Mother remarked.

Pappy spat at a toadstool ten feet away and hit it.

"Yes, ma'am," he said, "from Europe. Everything from

Europe. Nothing here was elegant enough. Maybe so. We ain't much for art in America, but I tell you, Miss Biddy, when we get ready for art, we'll make it ourselves."

Father appeared through the trees and waved. "This way!"

They gathered up their burdens and followed him to the old well.

"It's a little cluttered up with sycamore leaves," said Father. "But there's plenty of water."

In a little while they had fires crackling under three kettles, and the boys were drawing up more water for rinsing.

"This is a heap more trouble," said Mother, "but I must say it's more fun than doing the washing on board."

Between excursions into the little wood to hunt for firewood, the boys explored the island. They turned somersaults down the overgrown terrace, chased the dogs, played hide-and-seek among the crumbling walls, and picked sprays of purple lilacs from the straggling bushes in the deserted flower garden.

Finally the washing was done, and the clothes danced on a long line strung across the sunny lawn, propped up at intervals by forked poles.

"Now how about a rest, Miss Biddy?" said Father. "Let's find a comfortable spot under a tree."

"It's nicest in the orchard," Steve said. "Some of the apple trees are still in bloom and it smells elegant. There's long grass to lie down in."

Pappy went back to the boat to fetch Katy, and they all stretched out under an apple tree to listen to his music. Father lay on his back with his hands folded on his chest.

"I wish this were our own tree, growing in our own

orchard," he said dreamily. "Apple blossoms are the sweet-est of all."

Steve rolled over on his stomach and plucked a blade of grass to chew. Susan slapped at a fly that tried to settle on her nose. And Pappy went on playing soft old tunes.

Some time later, Father leaped to his feet sputtering and coughing.

"I swallowed a mouthful of confounded apple blossoms," he finally choked out.

"You hadn't ought to leave your trap door open when you fall asleep, George," said Pappy mildly. "Though by your own statement apple blossoms is the sweetest."

The boys laughed until they rolled in the grass, and Susan tittered.

"What sympathy!" said Father. "What feeling! Nothing but horselaughs, while their own father strangles to death before their eyes!"

"George," said Mother lazily, "now that you're on your feet, do you think you feel well enough to go and see if the clothes are dry?"

Father pretended to grumble as he walked away. In a few minutes he returned whistling.

"All hands on deck!" he cried. "I'm ashamed of you, lying around like this, when there's work to be done. Those clothes have been dry for at least an hour."

When everything had been gathered up and they started back to the boat with the dogs, Susan turned and gave one long look at the ruins.

"I still don't understand what happened here," she said thoughtfully. "When did the Blennerhassetts leave the island?"

"In 1807," Father answered.

"Well, I know ten years is a long time, but I don't see how everything could fall to pieces in ten years."

"It didn't fall to pieces," said Father. "It was destroyed."

"By whom?"

"Oh, by the militia, maybe the neighbors. The courts dismissed the case against Blennerhassett and Burr, but there was a lot of feeling against them. I've been told the militia fired their muskets into the walls, just to see the plaster fly."

Pappy wagged his head. "It don't do to get too uppish," he said. "It's agin nature in this country."

Chapter XVII

BAREFOOT BOYS

O N Saturday of the same week, as the storeboat was gliding along near the Ohio shore where the woods were fragrant with flowering locust, they were startled by a war whoop close at hand, followed by another farther away.

"Indians!" David said in a piercing whisper. "I'm going to get my sword."

Steve looked anxiously at Father.

"Man the oars," said Father. "Susan, you keep out of this."

The storeboat edged into shore, and Pappy jumped off alone to lash the boat to a projecting rock, then crept behind a buckeye bush.

Father signaled the boys to follow him ashore.

"Shouldn't I get my rifle?" Steve whispered.

Father shook his head and beckoned. David grabbed his sword and they went ashore quietly.

"My, you're brave, Father," David breathed.

"Ssh!" Father warned.

They crept from bush to bush up the steep bank. Then Father stood up and gave a war whoop.

"Halt, who goes there?" came a shrill voice.

"Friend!" Father yelled. "Come on, Pappy and the mighty tribe of Doaks!"

143

They charged out from their ambush, and found themselves facing a dark cave. In the entrance to the cave stood three barefoot boys with drawn bows, ready to shoot. They were fair-haired and blue-eyed, but each was painted with streaks of red clay and wore a turkey feather tied in his hair. A fourth boy raised his head above a sassafras bush a few feet away.

Father held up his right hand as a sign of peace and inquired gravely, "Have we the honor of addressing a great Indian chief?"

The boys grinned in their war paint. One of them spoke up. "Our chief's got the bilious fever and today's his day for a cold fit."

"Are you really Indians?" David asked with awe.

The boys gave him a disgusted look.

"Don't be silly, Dave," said Steve. "They're playing Indian."

"I was wondering," said Pappy, rubbing his jaw, "if Miss Biddy had any apple pie left from dinner. Seems to me I always heard Injuns was fond of pie."

"I've heard that too," Father agreed. "Is that the case with your tribe, boys?"

The four boys looked at each other and smiled until their war paint cracked.

"Do you want to see our cave?" asked the stoutest of the Indians. "They call it the Devil's Hole."

"Why?" asked David, putting his sword behind him.

"Well," Pappy said, "if it ain't the devil's hole, whose hole is it?"

The boys showed their visitors into the dark corners of their cave and brought out their collection of arrowheads,

colored rocks, the skeleton of a wildcat, a handful of por-
cupine quills, and an old rusty knife that might have been
left behind by river pirates in the early days. David showed
them his sword and told them its story.

Then, still carrying their little bows and arrows, the
four Indians trailed down the bank with the storeboat family, and climbed on board. Father took them down into the
kitchen and explained their needs to Mother.

As she cut the pie, she glanced at the mud-stained faces
of the four.

"Do Indians wash their faces before eating, like white
men?" she asked.

"No, no," said Father hastily. "That's not necessary when
they're on the warpath. But I reckon they do wash their
hands. Don't they, boys?"

The boys looked at their grimy hands and nodded. They
scrubbed in the tin basin, and wiped the rest of the dirt
off on the clean towel which Susan gave them.

While they were eating the apple pie, Father asked them
questions.

"Where do you live, boys?"

"Just a piece."

"How many miles?"

"Two, I reckon."

"Would your mother like to buy anything from the boat?"

"Don't know."

"Are you all brothers?"

"No. Cousins."

After they had finished and licked their fingers, Father
asked if they would like to ride home on the storeboat.

Their eyes shone, but the stout boy shook his head. "Can't.

We live about two miles from the river. Guess you can't take the boat through the woods."

"I guess not," Father admitted, laughing.

"But we'd admire to ride a piece with you and walk back," said another boy eagerly.

"All right."

All the boys sat on the roof and played mumbletypeg with Steve's knife while the boat left the shore and moved down the river. After half an hour, Pappy and Father steered for the shore, and the Indians started off on their long walk through the woods with war whoops.

Later that afternoon, Father shouted, "All hands on deck, and I mean all! We're coming to Letart's Rapids."

The whole family gathered on the roof.

"I'll steer," said Father. "Steve, you and Pappy man the sweeps. Susan, go down to the bows and man the gouger. Miss Biddy, you and David had better stand by to grab the sweeps if Steve and Pappy need help."

They took their posts quickly.

"Watch the channel near the right bank," Father snapped. "Stand to your places, but don't let your oars touch the water unless I give orders."

They began to hear the rush of the waters. Even the dogs seemed to feel the tension. They pattered up and down the narrow deck but did not bark. There was complete silence except for the churning of the water and a moo from Bessie.

Slowly the boat drifted toward the chute. The muscles in Father's arms and back bulged. The big boat creaked and shuddered as the swift current caught hold.

"Pull, Pappy!" barked Father. "She's swinging!"

Pappy lowered his sweep and pulled with a grunt. The boat straightened ánd kept her course.

Ahead of them at the end of the chute, a floating gristmill was anchored. Above the roar of the waters they could hear the squeaking of its great water wheel. As they came abreast of the mill, the storeboat began to slow down.

"We're running ashore here," said Father. "Put up your oars. It's resting time."

Pappy glanced back at the chute. "Mike Fink couldn't have done it better, George."

"I had good help," said Father.

The boat jarred a little against the bank. Steve jumped off and made her fast to a sycamore tree.

"Blow the horn, Dave," said Father. "There must be houses near by." He grinned at Mother. "I've navigated those rapids for ten years, but I never was nearer to getting the quiddles. I kept remembering it wasn't my own boat."

When David blew the horn, two bareheaded and barefoot boys came to the doorway of the scow which carried the machinery of the mill.

"Hello, the boat!"

"Hello, the mill!" Father shouted. "Have you got any corn meal to sell the boat?"

"None this time of year. But if you have any corn we can grind it."

Father turned to Susan. "How much have we?"

"Two sacks full."

"Let's have one sackful ground. Keep the other for the fowls."

Pappy helped Steve hoist the bag of corn to his shoulder

and trudged along the bank to the mill with him. The two miller boys seized the bag and dumped the corn into the hopper which fed the grindstones.

"Do you boys run the mill all by your lone?" Pappy asked.

The older boy looked up. "Yes. Our Dad has to take care of the farm. He's planting corn now."

Pappy looked out at an oak tree on the bank and nodded.

"It's time to plant corn," he said, "when the oak leaves are the size of a squirrel's ear."

When the meal was ground, the boys carefully measured it and set aside their own share as the price of the grinding.

On the way back to the storeboat, Steve and Pappy met the miller's wife, a rawboned woman in a blue sunbonnet and a loose wrapper.

"It's an elegant day, ma'am," Pappy remarked cheerfully.

"I've seen worse," said the miller's wife.

"Have you come to buy from the boat, ma'am?"

"If you've got any tin cups aboard the boat," she said sternly, "I'll buy. If you haven't, I won't waste my time."

"The finest tin cups this side of the Alleghenies, ma'am," said Pappy.

"I don't hanker after finery. I want plain tin cups."

Pappy dropped back and whispered to Steve, "I think she needs a little of Katy's singing."

As soon as they had deposited the bag of meal, Pappy tuned up the fiddle and began to play, while Steve and David hurried to the mill. The miller boys were skipping stones on the water when they joined them. There was a great deal of friendly and noisy rivalry, each boy trying to find the flattest stones and skip them the farthest.

After a while Father hallooed. Steve and David said good-by and ran back to the boat. The miller's wife was leaving, with a smile and an armful of purchases.

"I'm a plain-spoken woman," she was saying to Father, "and I don't lean to flattery. But it does my ears good to hear a pleasant word and a cheerful tune once in a while."

Three miles down the river, on the right shore, the store-boat passed the famous Rock of Antiquity.

"Can you see it?" asked Father, pointing. "That smooth big rock on the face of the bluff."

"I can't see very well," David complained. "Why can't we go ashore and climb up nearer?"

"Too many rocks and logs on the bank," said Father. "It's dangerous to try to land a big boat like ours."

"It looks like an Indian smoking a pipe," said Susan, "but the carving's so worn I can hardly tell."

"That's what it appears to be," said Father. "See, he's sitting with his elbows on his knees."

"I see him now!" said David.

"Who carved it, Father?" Steve asked.

"Nobody knows. Nobody even knows how long ago. It may be older than Mr. Tomlinson's Indian mound."

"It's things like that make me feel so young by compari-son," said Pappy, breaking into a jig.

The young Doaks began to jig too. Pappy grabbed his fiddle and swung into a hoe-down, and they all danced until Mother called up that it was time to make a landing for Saturday baths and supper.

Steve ran down to get a bar of yellow soap, but David

tore off his jacket and pantaloons and dived off into the water with a whoop.

Susan went below. "I wish I could at least go wading near the shore," she said enviously.

"Now, dear," said Mother, "you'd better just practice a little in the old tub while I fix supper."

When the boys came in to supper, they were clean and well brushed, but barefoot. Mother looked questioningly at their feet.

"Mother," said Steve, "we've decided not to wear shoes any more. Boys don't wear shoes in the West."

"That's all right," said Mother. "I reckon it will save shoe-leather."

Chapter XVIII

KENTUCKY IN SIGHT

FATHER passed by the next large town, which was Point Pleasant. He anchored the storeboat beyond the town at the mouth of the Great Kanawha river, where rafts and keelboats from the backwoods of Virginia swung into the Ohio.

Two rafts loaded with barrels of salt and one raft of lumber had passed with no more than a bellowed greeting. After half an hour of waiting for customers, Father began to grumble.

"I should have stopped in Point Pleasant," he said. "These boatmen don't want to buy anything."

"The trouble with you, George," said Pappy, "is you're spoiled. All the settlers in these parts live right on the river because there ain't any roads to speak of, and they all buy from the storeboat. It's got so you're in a flustration if you don't sell something every time you bat your eyes."

"I reckon you're right, Pappy. But I'd like to sail into port at Cincinnati with all the shelves as bare as the day we moved in."

Susan poked her head up through the hatchway. "We haven't any too much stock left, Father," she said. "It keeps me busy rearranging the shelves so they'll look full."

"I reckon you do too good a job," said Father. "I get

scared we're not selling enough. Well, let's shove off and try to reach Gallipolis tonight."

It was only four miles to Gallipolis, built high on the Ohio shore. But they were delayed by stops along the way, and did not reach the town until supper time.

Susan and the boys bolted their supper so that they might take a walk while it was still daylight. The last low shafts of sunlight were sifting through the trees when they leaped ashore and climbed the bank with Pappy and the dogs.

"See that column of gnats flying in the sun?" said Pappy. "That means fine weather."

The streets were almost deserted, and from every house came the smells of cooking. Occasionally they met a few stragglers hurrying home. Two men passed, deep in discussion.

David turned to stare after them. "What were they saying? I couldn't understand a word."

Pappy scratched his white head. "I reckon that was French, though it don't sound much like the French spoke by the Canadians on the river."

"Why do they talk French?" David asked.

"Those men? Because they're Frenchmen, and don't know no better."

Susan smiled. "Why shouldn't there be Frenchmen here? There are Germans in Pittsburgh."

"I can remember when there was nothing but Frenchmen in this town," said Pappy. "I never seen a more distressed crew. They paid for the land before they left France, but when they got here, they found they didn't own it. The scalawags who sold it to them had no more right than a stuffed buzzard. Some of them Frenchmen moved farther west, but a few of them stuck."

"It's a fine town now," Steve said. "Did they get their money back?"

"Not as far as I know," Pappy replied. "It cost them quite a few to clear their titles to the land."

"Aren't there any Americans here?" Susan asked. "I mean English-speaking ones."

"Plenty," said Pappy. "They moved in during the fuss."

David pointed to a handsome house set in elaborate gardens. Thriving vineyards stretched out behind the house as far as they could see.

"Whose house is that, Pappy?" he asked. "Is that where the mayor lives?"

"That house belongs to one of the Frenchmen," Pappy explained. "Twenty years ago he was a peddler."

They heard the barking of a dog and the drumming of hoofs on the hard dirt road. Brownie and Patch pricked up their ears.

"Hold them dogs!" Pappy cried.

Steve and Dave threw themselves on the dogs and held them fast. An immense flock of sheep pattered around a corner, herded by a big hairy dog. The shepherd followed, whistling a low tune. Brownie and Patch struggled and barked until the boys had to hold their muzzles.

"Whose sheep are them, stranger?" Pappy asked.

"They belong to everybody in town," the shepherd replied. "I take them to pasture every morning and bring them back in the evening."

"But how do you know which ones belong to whom?" Susan asked curiously.

"By the notches in their ears," the shepherd said. "Every sheep owner has his own way of notching, and it's registered with the county clerk." He caught one ewe as she passed and pointed out the little triangular nick that indicated her ownership.

"They look awful scrawny," David remarked.

"Scrawny nothing," said the shepherd. "They were sheared yesterday."

He turned and followed his flock. The sheep wavered down the street, sometimes running ahead, sometimes trying to make a dash for liberty on a side street. The shaggy dog was everywhere at once, growling and barking every time the sheep strayed from their path.

When they were out of sight, the boys released Patch and Brownie and started back to the boat.

The next morning a few customers wandered into the storeboat, more out of curiosity than need. But when they discovered that Father had books for sale, there was brisk trading. As one woman explained, there were no books in the four stores of Gallipolis, and no printing press.

David's face fell when he saw the last copy of *Robinson Crusoe* tucked under the arm of a plump smiling young woman. He plucked at Father's sleeve.

"Do you have to sell that one, Father?" he asked in a whisper. "I haven't finished it yet."

"Sorry, Bub," Father replied. "I'll buy you a copy of your own some day."

David scowled, and he went out on the roof to watch the chickens scratching in the straw on the deck below. He was still there, leaning against the flagstaff, when the storeboat pushed off for another lap of the journey.

The banks of the river were fairly well settled in this section of the West, but the farther they went, the fewer frame houses and the more log cabins they saw. And there were signs that the settlements did not extend very far inland—the frequent howling of wolves at night, and reeking bearskins tacked up on the cabin doors to dry.

One day they came upon a raft pinned on the rocks where it had been driven by the wind. Water was seeping through a gash in the deck, and the horses and people milled about, ankle deep in water.

"Looks like real trouble," said Father. "Let's run ashore and see what we can do."

After making the storeboat fast to shore, he and Pappy lowered the canoe and paddled over to the raft.

"Howdy, strangers," Father greeted them. "Need any help?"

"I calculate we do," a lean hatchet-faced man replied.

"How deep is it here?" Pappy asked, squinting down at the water.

"Not more than four feet, but it's deeper betwixt here and the shore."

Pappy peeled off his faded red calico shirt, and Father his blue gingham jacket and shirt.

"Everybody jump in," said Father. "We'll see if we can heave her off."

Father tied the canoe to the raft, and every man tumbled into the river. Steve dived from the storeboat and swam out to help. They pushed and lifted, but the raft did not budge.

"We'll have to unload her," said Father.

He made many trips back and forth with the canoe, depositing on shore all the women and children and movable cargo. Several of the raftsmen rode the horses off and forced them to swim to shore.

Then they heaved again at the stranded raft. This time it slid off the rocks. Pushing it before them, the men swam toward the bank and made a landing.

The damage was not serious. Two men chopped down an oak, others sawed it into sections, and within a few hours they had replaced the splintered floor boards with new ones. Meantime, Mother had made a big pot of hot tea and brought out a heaping plate of cold biscuits and a jar of apple butter. The children of the raft ate greedily, and now and then one of the men stopped his work to gulp a cup of tea.

"I reckon she's fixed now," said Father finally. "Let's get your plunder back on board."

The hatchet-faced man shook his head. "We're mighty obliged to you, stranger, but we can do that ourselves after we rest a while. It seems like we ought to buy something of you, after all your kindness. But we've only got the price of a few acres in the Illinois country."

"That's all right," said Father. "We had no ax to grind. We're always glad to help folks in trouble."

As soon as he and Pappy and Steve could change into dry clothes the storeboat set off once more.

A few days later, the storeboat came to the second stretch of straight river, beyond the mouth of the Great Guyandot. This time they could see for miles ahead, and distant craft looked like mere specks on the water.

One of these specks proved to be a small keelboat sailing upstream with its square sail billowing. As it approached,

Pappy turned the steering oar over to Steve and cupped his hands to his mouth.

"What's the news down river?" he yelled.

"Steamboat blew up near Point Coupee about the middle of April," came the reply.

Steve gasped. "Which one?" he shouted.

"Don't know exactly. Heard it was the 'Washington.' Busted her boilers and killed the passengers."

Father, sitting with his back against a rain barrel, caught sight of Steve's face and jumped to his feet.

"I'll take the oar, Red," he said kindly.

Steve swallowed and began to walk up and down the roof. Pappy shook his bony fist at the departing keelboat.

"Bandy-legged zanies!" he stormed. "Goggle-eyed fop-doodles! Can't they bring no better news than that?"

There was important news from the East the next day. The Ohio packet on its way down from Pittsburgh brought word that Congress had at last voted to build the Erie canal, fulfilling General Harrison's prophecy.

"Do you hear that?" Father cried. "Do you realize what that means to the settlements in the Northwest? Every village on the Great Lakes can send its goods by water to Europe, with only a short portage around Niagara Falls."

"Hold on, George," said Pappy sourly. "What the Great Lakes gain in trade, the Ohio loses."

"Oh, there's plenty for both," Father insisted. "This is a great country, Pappy."

Steve was still mournful. "I don't see what difference it makes, if Captain Shreve went down with his boat. Now I guess we'll never have free navigation."

"Those men may have been wrong," said Father. "Shreve may have escaped."

Steve could not be cheered. He sat down on the edge of the roof and stared vacantly at the water. But toward the end of the Long Stretch, where the river resumed its winding, he was jolted out of his gloom.

"Around the next bend," said Father, "is the real West, where Kentucky begins."

Steve looked up, scrambled to his feet and ran to the hatchway. "Mother! Susan!" he called down excitedly. "You'd better come up! We'll be in Kentucky pretty soon."

The womenfolks dropped everything and joined the others on the roof.

"It seems almost like the end of the journey, doesn't it?" said Mother.

"Where's the state line, Father?" David asked.

"The Big Sandy river is the dividing line. Do you want to catch a fish to celebrate, Bub?"

David grinned sheepishly. "Not this time, I guess."

As the storeboat approached the mouth of the Big Sandy, Steve pointed. "What are those patches of bright green?"

"That's cane-brake," Father explained. "It makes fine fodder for cattle and an elegant hiding place for bears."

"Once just about here," said Pappy, "I saw a log in the water and I pulled on the oar. But that danged log kept a-swimming right at me. It wan't no log at all. 'Twas a bear. 'Shoo!' says I. 'There ain't no room on this skiff for you and me both, Mr. Bear.' He took one look at me and agreed with me. He made off up river like a streak of lightning. Last I seen of him he was a-snorting round the bend."

"Why didn't you kill him?" asked David.

"What did I want with a bear, live or dead?" Pappy returned.

"Look at that!" Father exclaimed, nodding toward the Big Sandy river.

They could see the heads of four horses swimming across the Big Sandy toward Kentucky. Carried along behind them were six or seven men and women up to their waists in water and clinging grimly to one another.

"Must be a wagon somewhere underneath," remarked Pappy. "Pity they ain't got a watertight Conestoga that would float. Reminds me of a curious happening in Ohio."

They watched the struggle against the current. Finally the horses gained the shore and the wagon emerged from the water. The Doaks broke into cheers.

When the clamor had died down, Susan said, "Tell us about the curious happening, Pappy."

"Oh, yes. Well, it was in Ohio. There'd been a heap of rain, so's I couldn't tell exactly where the road was. I was a-floundering along, and pretty soon I seed an elegant beaver hat lying in a big mud puddle, crown upwards."

Pappy stopped and squinted at his listeners. "I thinks to myself I'd like to have such a hat. So I took my long whip and I flicked the hat over onto what was passing for dry land at the time. A man's head turned and scowled up at me from that there puddle."

The young people began to chuckle.

"He says," Pappy continued, "he says, 'Hello, stranger! Who told you to knock my hat off and uncover me to the rain?' So I says it appears to me he's in need of help."

"How did you get him out, Pappy?" David asked.

"I didn't. He says to me, 'Oh, never mind,' he says. 'I'm in rather a bad fix, it's true. But I have a good critter under me who has carried me through many a worse place than this.' So I up and left him."

"Pappy, you old liar," said Father, "take this steering oar before Miss Biddy washes your mouth out with yellow soap."

Chapter XIX

MAYSVILLE

THE daily lessons were discontinued early in June. To celebrate the last day of school, Mother called for recitations from her pupils, a speech from Father, and music from Pappy. Afterward the boys went swimming, and Susan went ashore at the first opportunity to pick a bowlful of red and yellow columbines "for teacher."

A few days later they reached Maysville, the first important town in Kentucky and one of the oldest landing places on the river. Father and Pappy brought the boat into Limestone Creek with some difficulty on account of low waters, and made her fast beside another storeboat which flew a tattered yellow flag.

Father and the other storemaster eyed each other and the two yellow flags at the bows.

Finally Father spoke up, with a friendly smile. "Howdy, stranger! I hope we're not going to get in each other's way. My name's Doak. I'm trading my way down river to turn this craft over to Riddle of Cincinnati."

"Howdy, Mr. Doak," the other returned with some cordiality. "Well, this is my own boat, such as it is. Name's Wilson."

They leaned out over the water to shake hands.

"Maybe we ought to dicker a little," Father suggested. "You take one side of the river and I'll take the other."

"Don't think that's necessary, Doak," said Wilson. "There's trade enough for both. You'll be moving on before I do. I put in at Maysville to lay in supplies for the late summer trade. The river'll be full of emigrants from Europe this year."

"How does he know?" asked David at Father's elbow.

Father explained. "Emigration has been increasing since the Napoleonic wars. We haven't seen any foreigners because most of the passenger ships don't even leave Europe till spring. They can't get as far west as this before late July."

Mother came up on the roof in her bonnet, swinging a basket and her reticule. "I'm going to the market," she said. "Does anybody want to come with me?"

Susan and the boys joined her, leaving Father and Pappy to watch the boat and keep the dogs in.

They found the market house easily enough. The stalls were fragrant with ripe strawberries, raspberries, cherries and currants, and piled high with greens of all sorts.

"My mouth is set for fresh fruit," said Mother. "I'm going to find it hard to be thrifty."

"Oh, don't try, Mother," Susan pleaded. "Everything looks so good."

Mother chose a big basket of strawberries and put it into her market basket. While she was paying for them, the boys reached in and took several berries.

At that moment there was a noise in the street outside. Voices shouted, "Hurry up!" Feet pounded the sidewalks. A cannon boomed.

Mother gave Steve a shove. "Run along and see what's happening."

Susan followed the boys, and they joined the running crowd.

"What's happening?" Steve asked breathlessly as they reached the waterfront.

Another cannon roared almost in their ears. Several women shrieked. Steve edged through the mob until he saw two tall masts above the heads of the people. There was another boom across the river.

"What's happening?" he asked of the nearest man.

"It's Mr. Zane's schooner, returned from New Orleans with a West India cargo."

"Do they do this every time a boat comes home?"

"No, but this one wasn't expected for another two weeks. She was gone only three months in all."

The tall dark sailors began to push through the crowd, shouting to all their friends.

David and Susan arrived at Steve's side, hot and disheveled.

"What a lot of people!" said Susan, pushing back a dark curl.

"Steve," said David, staring, "are all those sailors Indians?"

"No, silly. They're sunburned. You're almost as dark as they are, from being in the sun so much."

"Well, if you could see your freckles!" David jeered.

"Mine too," said Susan, covering her nose with her hand. "I hope Simon doesn't mind freckles."

"What did you say?"

"Nothing."

Further excitement was added by the arrival of the stagecoach on the large ferryboat, which was propelled by horses on a treadmill. The crowd parted to let the stagecoach roll off the ferry, and many willing hands reached out to steady the coach as the prancing chestnut horses hauled it up the bluff to the main street of Maysville.

Taking advantage of the gathering, a man in a black beaver hat, green jacket and fancy checked waistcoat elbowed his way through, giving out handbills.

Steve got one, and read the announcement aloud. There was to be a stage performance that evening, tickets one dollar. The program would include a comedy, a farce, tightrope dancing, and music by a Negro orchestra.

"Hurray!" cried David. "Let's make Father take us."

They hurried back to the storeboat, and Steve shoved the handbill into Father's hands.

"What does it say?" asked Pappy.

Steve explained.

"Please, Father, do take us," Susan begged.

He studied the announcement gravely. "A dollar apiece is a smart chance of money for one evening," he said.

Mother came back from market with all her bundles and her basket overflowing. She demanded to hear all about the commotion on the waterfront. After they had told her, the young people showed her the handbill.

"Oh, yes, I have one too," she said. "George, I was wondering." She looked up at Father and smiled.

"It costs too much," he said shortly.

"Now, George, we can save money some other way."

Pappy nodded agreement with her.

Father frowned. "I wish you wouldn't force me to argue in front of the children. You don't seem to understand that it's not simply a question of the money. This isn't Philadelphia, or even Pittsburgh. All the rough element will be there. I'm afraid the theater is no place for ladies and young folks."

Mother's eyes snapped. "George Doak, do you think the children and I can be corrupted by rough manners and bad language?"

Father squirmed. "I'm afraid you still don't understand, Biddy. I don't like to think of you among those rowdies."

Mother looked hard at him, and then smiled. "George, dear, we're not gentry. Don't try to protect us too much."

Father patted her cheek. "All right, Miss Biddy. We'll go."

The young people cheered and Pappy cackled.

"Now that that's settled," said Mother, "I want to show you the strange coins they gave me at the market house."

She opened her reticule and poured out several small fragments of coins.

"Cut money!" Father exclaimed. "I haven't seen much of that lately. I guess Maysville gets it in trade with the back country."

The young people examined the cut money curiously.

"They're pieces of silver dollars!" said Susan.

"That's right," said Father. "Money has always been pretty scarce in the backwoods, especially smaller coins. So folks make change by chopping dollars into halves, quarters, or eighths. Let's take another look at this cut money of yours, Miss Biddy. We must be sure nobody has been making five quarters out of a dollar."

"I asked questions at the market house," said Mother, "and I took care we weren't cheated."

That evening there was a great deal of scrubbing of faces and shining of shoes with bacon grease.

"I'll have no bare feet tonight," Mother had said.

The boys groaned, but dutifully put on their shoes and clumped about as if they had never worn them before. When everyone was ready to go, Father locked the kitchen door and the hatchway against river thieves, and they set out for the frame building where the entertainment was to be given.

As they walked along, Pappy cocked his head at the evening sky. "Yellow sunset," he remarked. "And do you see how low them swallows is flying? We're going to have rain, and it's about time. The river smells bad."

Although it was early when they reached the hall, most of the benches were already taken. Steve, Pappy and David found seats near the front of the house, while Mother, Father and Susan slipped into seats at the rear.

The hall was lighted by burning pine knots. A haze of smoke from these torches and from the cigars of the men almost obscured the wrinkled curtains drawn before the stage, and billowed in clouds toward the ceiling.

The audience was made up largely of men. There were boatmen in red shirts, townsmen in homespun or calico pantaloons with bright calico shirts, and a few backwoodsmen wearing leather or homespun suits and moccasins. They roared greetings to one another, hurled insults across the hall, and finally began to stamp their feet with impatience.

The stamping increased until the hall began to rock. At length the curtains parted and the handbill distributor came out.

"Ladies and gentlemen," he began.

He was interrupted by a chorus of boos.

"We don't want no speeches, Limey," someone shouted. "We paid our money to see the show!"

Others took up the cry. "Give us the show!"

Mother leaned over and asked Father why the man was called Limey.

"It's the name for any Englishman," said Father, "because English sailors are fed lime juice to keep away scurvy."

The man opened his mouth several times to speak, but he was drowned out by the shouts of the audience. He withdrew, and there was another long wait.

"What do you suppose he was trying to say?" Mother asked.

"Oh, he was probably going to tell us that there'd be a delay," said Father. "These little troupes have a hard time keeping up with their trappings from one village to the next."

At last the curtains were drawn aside, and the show began. The first part was an English comedy called "The Honeymoon." It was the story of a handsome but ill-tempered young bride who was tamed by her husband. The audience entered into the play by shouting encouragement to the husband.

"Hit her!"

"Turn her up and spank her!"

"Treat her like a stubborn critter! That's the only way to handle a woman!"

Father stole a glance at Mother. "Do you still think you ought to have come?"

"Hush, George! I'm enjoying it."

When the subdued bride acknowledged her defeat at the end of the comedy, bellows of approval filled the hall.

During the intermission, a Negro band came out before the curtains and played two different tunes at the same time, on two complete sets of fiddles, triangles, and banjos. The rough audience rocked and stamped their feet with the music. The Negroes rolled their eyes and grinned.

Next came a piece entitled " 'Tis All a Farce." The actors wore false noses and slapped each other down with clattering sticks. The more the actors tumbled about the stage, the more the audience roared with laughter. Mother and Susan found themselves shrieking as loudly as the rest.

The conclusion of the entertainment was the tightrope dance. When the dancer proved to be the ill-tempered bride of the first piece, the men in the audience began to tease her unmercifully.

"I wouldn't let my wife do that!" a hoarse voice bawled.

Amid the shouts and laughter of the spectators, she finished the act and leaped lightly down. The show was over.

Almost to a man, the audience swarmed out of the smoky hall and made for the tavern. Father was surprised to find Pappy beside him as they walked back to the dark waterfront.

"What! no tavern?" he asked.

"I'm saving up," said Pappy. "Besides, there's too many boatmen around. 'Tain't safe for my rheumatism."

Chapter XX

BAD WEATHER

THE next day the dawn spread slowly over a sky banked with black clouds. While the boys were waiting for Susan to finish washing at the basin by the window, a streak of lightning licked at the hills and a clap of thunder made the crockery rattle on the shelves.

Then the rain began. Big raindrops drummed on the roof of the storeboat and beat at the windowpanes on first one side and then the other. The peals of thunder were so loud and so prolonged that Brownie and Patch cowered under the kitchen table, Bessie kept to her shed, and the chickens and geese murmured uneasily.

"Well, we can't leave Maysville now," said Father over his bacon and eggs. "It would be flying in the face of Providence."

As the day passed, the thunder and lightning lessened, but the rain pelted down relentlessly. Beyond Limestone Creek, the wind swirled and whipped the big river into whitecaps.

More and more skiffs, flatboats, rafts and keelboats took refuge in the rising creek and along the river bank. All day the Doaks heard the sound of hand-pumps discharging the water from the big boats. On the smaller boats men and boys bailed out their flooded craft with buckets and dippers.

The snug storeboat had many visitors. A hatter, a shoemaker and a tailor returning to Pennsylvania from a walking tour through Ohio came in to dry their drenched coats beside the kitchen stove.

"Times are good in the West," they reported. "There's work for any man with a skill. We stopped in every village to work for our board, and we're going home with money in our pockets."

Two flatboatmen, on their way home to Brownsville with their knapsacks full of New Orleans money, brought Father the news that a famous bandit had at last been captured on the Natchez Trace. Later in the day a flashily dressed man whose business was swapping horses sidled up to Father and tried in vain to persuade him to lay a bet on a horse race to take place at five o'clock if the rain permitted.

There were also customers from the various craft along the banks. Mother and Susan were kept busy scrubbing away their muddy footprints in the store.

Toward evening a keelboat patroon named Peters came to see Father and Pappy. David watched with openmouthed admiration every move the big man made.

"I had to stop over here in Maysville anyway, rain or shine," said Mr. Peters. "We had adverse winds all the way up from the Falls. Couldn't use the sails or poles, so we had to use the cordelle all the way."

"What's a cordelle?" asked David.

"And you a keelboatman!" said Father. "Don't you know that's a towrope?"

"I guess I disremembered," said David.

"My men ain't used to tramping through bushes and rocks," Mr. Peters resumed. "Their feet got sore, the ropes blistered their paws, and pretty soon they began to grumble.

Said they hadn't been hired to walk all the way to Wheeling where we're bound. So I had to give them a rest here."

The rain continued steadily for two days, and still the boats gathered. A small storeboat flying a bedraggled red flag headed up the creek with a challenging toot at the Doaks' yellow flag.

Now and then Pappy put on his old blue jerkin and wandered off to the town for a game of billiards. Just before supper on the second day, he burst into the kitchen, sputtering with news. His hair and faded red shirt were soaked with rain, but he had Katy wrapped up in his jerkin to keep dry.

"Keelboat just got in from New Orleans!" he panted. "'Twan't the 'Washington' blew up, but the 'Constitution.'"

The storeboat resounded with cheers and questions.

"It was like this," Pappy went on when he had got his breath. "The 'Constitution' was overtook by the 'Washington,' and her captain, a man by the name of Guird, tried to race the 'Washington' and overtaxed his boilers."

"He should have known better," said Steve gleefully.

"He learned too late," said Pappy, shaking his head.

"Let's have a tune to celebrate," Mother suggested.

"Can't," said Pappy. "I got business to attend to. Man I know on that keelboat."

"Not Wilkins!" Father laid a restraining hand on Pappy's wet shoulder.

"Wilkins himself," said Pappy. "Turn me loose, George."

Mother interposed. "Please, Pappy, don't get hurt."

"Wilkins ain't wearing the red feather no more," said Pappy. "Ain't that a sign I can lick him?"

The old man flapped his arms, threw back his head and crowed like a game rooster, and with an excited chuckle dashed out into the rain again.

Supper was a silent meal, and in every face was the same uneasiness. Pappy did not return in time to eat with them, nor by the time the dishes were washed.

Mother finally said, "George, don't you think you ought to find out what's happening? Somebody ought to help Pappy. He's not so young as he acts."

Father shook his head. "I've seen Pappy in a rough and tumble. He may not be young, but he can whip half a dozen Wilkinses. If I put in my oar, every boatman in town would take sides and there'd be a real battle. You don't think I want to sit here and wait, do you?"

"Let me go," pleaded Steve. "I promise not to interfere, but I can at least see what's going on."

"No. Get to bed, all of you," said Father. "Pappy will be back before morning, I'm certain."

But there was little sleep for any of them that night. The boys and Susan lay awake for hours, wondering and talking, and at length dropped off into restless dozing.

They jumped out of their beds and dressed in the gray light of dawn. There was a faint tinge of pink above the mass of clouds at the horizon, and the rain had stopped. When they came into the kitchen, they found Father asleep with his head on the table. Mother was quietly making a fire in the stove.

"Pappy didn't get home at all last night," she whispered. "And your father never went to bed."

In shocked silence the three young people washed their faces and tiptoed around the room. After a while the coffee began to simmer in the crock at the back of the stove. Mother dipped out a cupful and set it down before Father.

"George," she said softly, shaking his shoulder, "wake up and drink this."

He stirred and opened his eyes. "Where's Pappy?" he asked. "I heard him come in after you went to bed, but I was too sleepy to move."

"He's not here," said Mother. "His bedding wasn't even unrolled."

Father sprang to his feet, suddenly wide awake. "I won't stop for coffee now," he said, putting on his blue gingham jacket. "I'm going to take a look around."

They heard him stride through the hall and clamber up the ladder.

Mother opened the windows to admit the fresh cool air and looked out. The sky was clearing and the clouds were scattering. On many of the boats up and down the creek, she saw women wringing out clothes and spreading their damp bedding to dry. She sighed and turned away.

"Eat your breakfast, children," she said in a calm voice. "I guess we'll leave Maysville as soon as your father finds Pappy, if he's not too badly hurt."

Steve laid down his knife and fork. "I'm not very hungry."

"Neither am I," said Susan. "I keep worrying."

David's lip began to quiver.

"All right," said Mother. "Let's put the plates in the oven to keep warm. We'll all wait for Pappy."

"Well, anyway," said Steve, with an attempt at a grin, "Pappy won't have to hunt for Wilkins any more."

Susan got up from the table and went into the store to tidy the shelves a bit. She stopped short at the door.

"Mother!" she called out.

Startled by her tone, Mother ran down the little hallway. The boys pattered after her.

Susan pointed to the money box on the counter. "I forgot to lock it and put it under the featherbeds last night."

Mother hurried over and looked in the box. "Why, it's empty!"

Susan began to cry. "Oh, I've tried so hard to remember it every night, and the one time I forgot—"

Mother put her arms around her.

"Let's not worry, child. Maybe your father took the money, in case he has to pay a fine for Pappy."

David started to say something, but Mother hushed him with a glance. Steve patted his sister's shoulder awkwardly and led her back to the kitchen where they all sat down to wait.

It seemed hours before Father came back, and he came alone, dragging his feet.

"Didn't you find Pappy?"

"No. I've been to the jail, and I've asked at all the taverns. Everybody saw him last night asking for Wilkins."

"Did he find him?"

"I don't know," said Father wearily. "Wilkins didn't go back to his boat last night. One bartender said he overheard Wilkins bargaining for a horse, and the sheriff tells me a horse was stolen outside that same tavern."

He threw himself in a chair and leaned his elbows on the table.

"It looks to me," he said, "as though Pappy has gone chasing after Wilkins, and we'll have to wait till he comes back."

Mother laid her hand on his arm. "George, did you take the storeboat money when you went out this morning?"

Father stared at her. "No, Biddy. What's happened?"

Susan began to cry again, and even Steve blew his nose. Mother showed Father the empty money box.

His mouth set grimly and his eyes turned a hard gray. "So that's what I heard last night," he said shortly. "I never thought Pappy would do a thing like that."

"How can you be so sure it was Pappy?" Mother asked.

"Who else could it be? He knows how much we had. The money's gone and Pappy's gone. You must admit it looks strange."

Mother bit her lip.

"Every cent gone," said Father bitterly. "Nothing left but our bank draft. How much was there, Susan?"

The girl ran to get her books, and came back crying harder than ever. "Three—three thousand, four hundred and twelve dollars and fifty cents."

"That's even more than I thought," he said, shaking his head. "Well, our bank draft will cover Mr. Riddle's share. But it means nothing left for us, no land, no house. And I reckon I'll have to go back to the river."

David tried manfully to keep back the tears, but finally gave way in a loud wail.

Mother sat down beside Father and took his hand. "George, we've had hard times before, and we'll have them again. Let's not give way to our feelings."

Susan could only sob, over and over, "It's all my fault, it's all my fault."

Father pushed back his chair and stood up. "Let's stop this sniveling."

"Are you going to notify the sheriff?" Mother asked anxiously.

Father clenched his fists. "Yes, by heaven, I'll do that. Why should we pay for somebody else's dishonesty?"

Mother slowly shook her head. "I'd as soon have Steve arrested."

He stared at her. "Even after what he's done to us?"

"We don't know why he did it," she said. "Maybe he needed money badly, and didn't want to tell you."

Father walked out of the room and climbed up to the roof, where they heard him pacing up and down.

"We have bacon, potatoes, flour, corn meal, sugar, coffee, and more eggs, milk and butter than we can use," Mother said. "Davie, you must catch plenty of fish. Maybe we can sell some."

Father reappeared in the doorway. "I reckon you're right, Biddy. Come on, boys, let's shove off before anything else happens. We're shorthanded now. You'll both have to help. You too, Susie, and for heaven's sake stop blaming yourself."

With heavy hearts the young people followed him to the roof and took their places at the sweeps.

"Push off! Easy there!"

With some bumping against their neighbors, they finally guided the storeboat out of the creek and into the main current of the river. There was no cheerful good-by toot on the horn this time, and no exchange of compliments with the other boatmen making ready to leave the landing place.

As soon as she could put up her sweep, Susan went below to see if Mother needed any help in the kitchen. David soberly resumed his fishing. Father and Steve were left alone on the roof to steer the boat in silence. In the oven, four plates of forgotten breakfast toasted to a crisp.

Chapter XXI

LONG DAYS

MOST of the fun had gone out of the voyage down the river. Without Pappy to entertain them with his dry jokes and stories and Katy's cheerful music, they no longer hurried through their chores to gather on the roof.

Nobody else could yell friendly insults at passing boats with Pappy's fervor. Although they met more than usual, they let many a craft slip by with only a halfhearted wave of the hand.

Steve's back and shoulders ached from long hours at the steering oar, but he was too proud to tell Father. Forgetful of his turn at the oar, Father sat hour after hour, staring at the water.

The steering itself was not hard, because the waters were rising steadily as a result of the rains. There was no danger of foundering. Steve held on to the oar grimly, although the glare from the water blinded him and the hot roof blistered his bare feet.

David fished until he ran out of bait. After that he jumped ashore every time the boat made a landing, and dug for angleworms along the edge of a potato patch or a corn field. Sometimes he sold his catch to other boats or to the settlers. More often the Doaks ate fish for breakfast, fish for dinner, and fish for supper.

One fine June day a rude skiff with a shed in the middle came alongside. There was no one on board except a frail gray-headed old couple, who were tugging at the oars with all the energy of a pair of youngsters.

Father looked down at them and smiled for the first time in many days.

"Where's your crew?" he asked them.

The old couple rested on their oars and looked up.

"Don't need any," replied the old man.

"Where are you bound?"

"Illinois. The old woman and me felt sort of lonesome after the children got married and started bustling for themselves. So we thought we'd follow them out to the back lands and try our luck."

"Hold on a moment!" Father cried.

He vaulted down the hatchway and came back in a few seconds with a bundle wrapped in a new red bandanna handkerchief. He flung it to the skiff.

"May health and prosperity travel with you, friends," he said.

The woman put up her oar and reached for the bundle.

"Thank you kindly, sir. We wish you Godspeed."

David ran along the narrow deck and shouted, "Do you want any fish?"

The old couple nodded vigorously. The boy tossed them his entire string of fish. With smiles and nods the two old people took up their oars again and were soon out of sight.

"That was a thoughtful thing to do, Davie," said Father.

"I'll catch lots more," said David. "What did you give them, Father?"

"Oh, some tea and a couple of fishhooks and a few other

nicknacks. I know we can't spare the money, but they looked worse off than we do."

Father sat down on the edge of the roof again. Suddenly the smile faded from his face and he leaped to his feet.

"By all the stuffed alligators in Kaskaskia!" he said. "If those two old folks can start a new life at their age, so can we. I'm going to stop this moping. Steve, give me that oar. You must be pretty much used up."

The boy stretched his tired muscles and lay down on the warm roof face downward. After a while he rose up on his elbows and yawned.

"Smoke in the woods on the Ohio side," he observed.

Father glanced down at David fishing on the deck below. He waited until the boy had landed a small perch.

"If you can leave off fishing, Bub, I reckon it's time to blow the horn," he said.

David puffed out his cheeks and sounded a great blast, while Steve and Father ran the storeboat ashore.

They found that the thick smoke came from a crackling bonfire of green underbrush in a small clearing. About a dozen men moved about in the surrounding woods, hacking their way through the tangled creepers. Axes rang against the great trunks of trees, cowbells tinkled, dogs bayed in the distance, and the men shouted as they worked.

"Looks like a house-raising frolic," Father remarked. "In the West the neighbors come in and help a man clear his land, build a house, plow his fields, pick wool, husk corn, make quilts. After the work is done, there's a barbecue or a feast brought in by the womenfolks. Then comes the frolic, with games, contests, and square dances."

"Will there be a frolic when we build our house?" Steve asked.

Father shook his head. "I doubt that. Folks aren't quite so neighborly near the big cities."

They both started and looked at each other.

"I—I forgot," Steve stammered. "There ain't going to be any house for a long time."

Father frowned. "Let's stop thinking about it, Stevie. Come, if these folks are too busy to come to the storeboat, we can take time to go ashore. Make her fast, Steve."

"I'm going too, Father," David said.

They jumped off the boat and strolled up to the nearest group of men, who were chopping deep notches in the logs as fast as others dragged them over from the woods. Their faces were streaked with soot and perspiration.

One of the men looked up. "Howdy, strangers. Come to join the house-raising?"

"I'm afraid we can't stay long," said Father. "Is that your house going up?"

The man straightened up and nodded proudly. "A whole half section of the finest bottom land in Ohio. And if the frolic will hold out three or four days, I'll have me a double cabin with a breezeway between."

He waved his hand toward the other workers. Off beyond the clearing, some were cutting down trees, others were lopping off the branches, and still another group were measuring the ground where the house was to be built. One man brought an armload of green branches and threw it on the fire.

"Do you need any hardware?" asked Father, blinking as

the wind blew the smoke toward him. "We have nails, hinges and such stuff aboard the boat."

The man scratched his stubble of a beard. "If I'd known you had hardware aboard I might have paid some attention to your horn. When I saw the yellow flag I figured you had nothing but dry goods for the womenfolks. But I don't know if I can buy. Land office took pretty near every dollar I had. Guess I do need some hinges for my doors, though."

While Father and the settler went on board to choose several sets of hinges, Steve and David watched the workmen. The men had finished measuring the cabin site, and they began to roll the logs over and hoist them into place. The notches matched at the corners, so that the logs fitted into place, one above the other.

"There's big cracks between the logs," David remarked. "Won't it be cold in the winter?"

"Oh, he'll fill up the cracks with mud," Steve explained.

Three of the walls rose to a height of four feet or more before their very eyes, and the boys were reluctant to leave when Father called them.

"We ought to stay, Father," Steve protested. "If they'd let us help, we could learn how to build a cabin and it wouldn't cost anything."

"Stand to your sweeps there, boys," said Father firmly. "We have to get a piece on our way and sell the rest of Mr. Riddle's goods. We can't even buy our land now."

Another sunny day a bearded man paddled out from the Kentucky shore in a rough canoe.

"I'll trade honey for a Barlow knife," he announced.

"What do you ask for honey?" Father asked.

"Seventy-five cents a gallon."

"You won't get much of a knife at that price, stranger," said Father, "but I'll show you what I have."

While the man was in the store, there were shouts and a clatter on the shore.

Steve leaned over the hatchway. "Father, come and see! There's a crowd of ladies on shore pounding on kettles and ringing cowbells and hollering like all get-out."

"It's nothing," said the bearded man. "It's only my womenfolks charming the bees to a new hive. The queen bee commenced to hum yesterday evening and they swarmed this morning."

There were few towns along this stretch of the river, and the woods were tangled with vines and thick with under-brush. The storeboat made brief stops at Charlestown and Augusta, both on the Kentucky side, but as usual found the best trading among the farms and smaller settlements.

One morning toward the third week in June the sun rose dark red in a dappled sky. When Father saw it from the kitchen window he shook his head uneasily.

"Storm's coming," he said. "I thought the fish were leaping too much last night at twilight."

All morning on the roof he slapped at the flies that were stinging his bare arms, and watched the clouds gather until they hid the pale sun.

At noon the storm began, not with gentle showers, but with driving rains and high winds. Father called the entire family to help him make a harbor against the wind, and there they stayed for two days.

On one side of them the river was rough with whitecaps, and on the other the tree tops swayed and creaked in the wind. Peepers and tree frogs kept up such a din that they could not hear the ticking of the clock. Now and then there came a low threatening rumble of thunder that sent the dogs whimpering into dark corners. The muggy heat inside was stifling, and the candles had to be lighted in the middle of the afternoon.

While they waited for the storm to abate, Steve made sketch after sketch of steamboats and rubbed them off the slate before they were finished. Susan cleaned, swept, dusted, scrubbed floors, and mended clothes until Mother began to worry about her. Then she set to work on her grass bonnet. She braided the grasses, pressed the braids flat and whipped them together, and the hat was done. But she laid it away without ribbons or flowers and forgot about it.

Father checked the accounts, listed the remaining stock, and estimated how much it might bring. Mother helped him for a few hours, then went into the bedroom to look for signs of mildew among the linens packed away. Father continued to set down columns of figures on the slate, and then absent-mindedly drew little arrows and Indian heads between the columns.

David ranged restlessly up and down the boat, watching first Father, then Steve, then Susan, and Mother. Whenever the rain slackened, he dashed out to fish until he was driven inside by a fresh downpour.

Every morning the river was a few inches higher. On the third day Father grew impatient, and in spite of the drizzling rain, steered the boat out from the shore. But they made poor progress against the wind, and there was danger of damage to the boat from floating logs, branches, and even uprooted trees which had begun to drift down the river.

Now and then backwoods boys darted out from the shore in canoes to pick up the drifting logs. They seized the logs with grappling hooks and skillfully steered them back to the bank.

After a large willow tree had floated past the storeboat, barely missing the stern, Father called his crew and headed for the muddy bank. He went ashore in the rain and chopped down two straight saplings. He stripped them of their branches, and gave one pole to Susan and the other to David.

"Susan, you go down to the bows," he said. "You'd better stand on the ledge outside the pen if you can keep from falling overboard. Use your pole to push away any floating timber that threatens the boat. Davie, you do the same at the stern."

Susan put on her plaid spencer and tied a bandanna over her curls, and she and David took their places. With this assistance Father and Steve kept a straight course down the river.

After a while the rain stopped and there was a yellow glow in the sky and on the water. Their clothes began to dry in streaks on their backs, and the chickens and geese stepped gingerly out of the shed to hunt for corn in the soggy straw. Father broke into a cheerful whistle.

David shrieked. "There's something coming that looks like a little shanty! It'll hit us!"

Father looked back over his shoulder and gave a sharp twist to the steering oar. The storeboat swung aside as the upturned shanty swirled past them.

"This is a real flood," Father remarked. "I don't remember a worse one."

"Maybe it'll go on for thirty days," offered David hopefully.

Father squinted up at the sky. "More thunderclouds," he growled. "At this rate it'll take us two weeks to get to Cincinnati, though we can't be more than twelve miles away."

"Only twelve miles!" Steve began to jig on the roof.

"We haven't sold all our stock," wailed Susan.

"I know," said Father, "but it's useless to try to trade any more. If a lady comes aboard and asks for pink calico, I have to persuade her to take yellow because we haven't any more pink."

Steve laughed. "If a man wants nails, you can offer him fishhooks, and a hammer to straighten them with. If he wants jean to make a coat, give him writing paper and tell him it sheds water better."

There was a sudden clap of thunder and big raindrops began to fall.

"We'll have to make another confounded landing," said Father. "Stand to your sweep, Red. Come along, Susan, we need you. If this pesky rain don't stop soon I'm going to lose my temper."

Susan made her way along the deck and climbed to the roof. She and Steve took their places, and the boat headed for the shore. David jumped down and made her fast to a beech tree.

"Shall I blow the horn, Father?" he asked, as he clambered back on board.

"There's not much use," said Father. "We have so little left to sell, and I don't see any houses."

"I'll blow it anyway," said David, and he did.

They waited below for several hours until the rain died down. Then when David sprang ashore to loosen the fasts, he almost collided with a spectacled old woman carrying a large spray of wild roses sprinkled with raindrops.

"Excuse me, ma'am," he said.

"Oh, my! You're not leaving, are you?" she said.

"Yes, ma'am. Did you want to buy something from the boat?"

"Well," she said, "I can't even buy a wooden nutmeg. But I wondered if the boat could spare something like a goose quill."

"We have plenty of goose quills," Father called down from the roof. "We raise our own." He pointed to the pen at the bows.

The old woman beamed through her spectacles. "That's fine," she said. "I've been trying to write with buzzard quills, but they're very unsatisfactory for fine writing. My brother in England couldn't even read my last letter."

"Wouldn't you prefer one of the new steel pens they're making in Pittsburgh now?" asked Father.

She pursed her lips. "I don't hold with those newfangled imitations," she said. "Goose quills are good enough for me. Mind you, though, I haven't any money."

Father laughed. "If you'll wait just a moment, I'll get you half a dozen quills. Have you a penknife to sharpen them?"

"I have, storemaster."

Father jumped down into the pen. The geese squawked,

the chickens protested, and the dogs barked, but he came back with a handful of white quills.

"And while you're here," said the old woman, "have you a clock aboard the boat?"

"One of Eli Terry's best," said Father.

"I'll thank you for the time of day," she said. "My clock stopped three days ago, and I've had nary a chance to set it, what with the rains and no sun in the sky."

David ran down to consult the clock and came back with the information that it was ten minutes past four. The old woman thanked him ceremoniously and presented Father with the bouquet of wild roses. Then she bustled off through the dripping woods, repeating to herself: "Ten minutes past four, ten minutes past four, ten minutes past four."

As they headed for the channel again, Father grinned.

"For all we know," he said, "that may be our last sale. Our first brought us a gold eagle, and our last a bunch of pink roses."

Chapter XXII

CINCINNATI AND A SCHOONER

AND still it rained. Between showers the storeboat edged from one sheltered cove to another, each time a little closer to Cincinnati. David continued to blow the horn whenever they spied a house, but Father had to stop the customers at the landing.

"Don't trouble yourself to come aboard the boat," he would say, "unless you happen to want one Barlow knife, a pocket compass, a speller, a pair of pewter candlesticks, a scythe, a pair of men's shoes, a bottle of bitters, a green glass bowl, six needles, a dozen fishhooks, five yards of yellow calico, two yards of cream-colored chintz with purple roses, or a fine English leghorn poke bonnet. That's all we have left."

And so the farmers and their wives would go away either indignant because they could not buy anything, or laughing at the idea of a storeboat without any store.

At last, early in the morning of Thursday, July third, the sun broke through the clouds. When he saw the first shaft of sunlight sparkling on the river, Father jumped up from the breakfast table.

"No more stops," he said briskly. "We've got only three or four miles to go. Make haste, boys."

Still fending off the debris that drifted by, they floated past tiny settlements of log houses and straggling farms where the sunlight glanced off the smooth green blades of growing corn and the warm breeze rippled through the yellow fields of rye and hay. On the Kentucky side, blue jays and parakeets flashed in and out among the trees hung with wild grapevines, and songbirds teetered on the slender branches of the bushes at the water's edge.

As the hot sun climbed high in the sky, the storeboat came within sight of the waterfront of Cincinnati. A steam mill towered above the boats at the water line, and the broad streets ran downhill to the river's edge. All the family stood on the roof shading their eyes to watch as they drew near. Across the Ohio they could see the little Kentucky towns of Newport and Covington shimmering in the sunlight.

Like Pittsburgh, Cincinnati had no docks, and the shore was ragged, muddy, and rutted with the tracks of wagon wheels. Yet the entire waterfront was crowded with schooners, barges, broadhorns, keelboats, family rafts, and largest of all, a long slate blue boat with one funnel and uncovered side-wheels.

"That's a steamboat!" Steve shouted. "Who is she?"

"Must be the 'General Pike,'" Father answered, "the one General Harrison's son has an interest in."

Steve studied the steamboat as they drifted past it. "She looks like a Fulton boat."

"I reckon she is, Red. The General said she was to be built by Captain Bliss of Connecticut, one of Fulton's associates."

"Low-pressure boilers, I guess," Steve said.

They located a space between a barge and a Kentucky boat, and with the help of the entire family Father steered the storeboat into the opening.

"Well, I reckon we're here," he said. "Jump down there, Dave, and tie her to that stake."

David was so excited that in leaping to shore he slipped, and slithered into the mud up to his bare calves, but he looked up and grinned.

"I guess I got a dose of slippery elm!" he said, as he fumbled with the rope.

Steve put up his sweep and wiped his hands on his pantaloons. "May I go and look at the 'General Pike,' Father?" he asked.

Father mopped his sunburned face with his bandanna and hitched up his pantaloons. "I think I'd rather you'd all wait here," he said. "Susan, get me the account books, the money box, and my bank draft. The sooner I see Mr. Riddle the better, though I don't look forward to it."

They watched Father tramp up the waterfront with the black ledgers and the big box under his arm.

"Let's hope Mr. Riddle isn't too hard on him," Mother said. "Well, while we're waiting, we might as well work."

"I don't feel like working," said Steve. "I'd like to run or holler or something. I feel like a boiler that's going to explode any minute."

"Well, suppose you try exploding the water out of these rain barrels," Mother suggested. "We'll need them to pack the crockery."

"Pack?" David wailed. "Do we have to get off the store-boat right away?"

"I fancy Mr. Riddle won't want the boat lying here in the harbor indefinitely," said Mother. "It isn't ours any longer. So let's be as cheerful as we can about leaving it."

"Where are we going to live, if we haven't a house?"

David asked. "What'll we do with Bessie and the chickens and the geese?"

"We don't know yet," said Mother.

She and Susan went below. As they walked through the store, Susan cast a glance at the little poke bonnet on a shelf by itself, still unsold.

"Stop hankering after that bonnet," Mother said. "It belongs to Mr. Riddle."

"I know," Susan said sadly.

They moved the empty trunk and the portmanteaus out into the kitchen where they could be reached, and began to take things out of the chests of drawers.

Susan looked up from a lawn petticoat she was folding. "I wish we didn't ever have to leave the storeboat," she said. "I dread the hard times ahead of us."

"So do we all," said Mother. "But at least Cincinnati is cleaner than Pittsburgh. They don't burn pit-coal here."

The boys rolled the empty barrels noisily down the hallway and set them up on the kitchen floor.

"Thank you, boys," said Mother. "Have you left anything on deck? Knives, fishhooks, or caps?"

Steve and David made a tour of the boat and came back with several articles.

"Now set aside enough plates, cups and tableware for dinner and supper," said Mother, "and you can start packing the rest of the crockery. Lay blankets between the layers to keep them from breaking. The blankets have got to be washed anyway."

They worked steadily for an hour or two, stopping occasionally to cool their faces in the wash basin. Above the clatter of dishes they could hear voices and the rattle of wagons along the waterfront.

At length Father returned. His step was springy and he was smiling.

"Riddle is a mighty fine man," he said. "At first he didn't want to accept my bank draft. Said I could pay him off a little at a time. But I insisted, because I don't like to be indebted to anybody."

Mother nodded with satisfaction.

"In spite of everything," Father continued, rubbing his hands, "we're nearly three hundred dollars ahead, besides forty-two dollars in coin left over from the housekeeping money. That will keep you all nicely while I run down to New Orleans with a cargo."

"Nevertheless," said Mother, "I don't aim to be idle. I'm going to teach school. This voyage has spoiled us, George. We can't wait another ten years for our own home."

"I'll find work as a sewing woman, Father," said Susan quietly.

Father frowned. "You're both talking fiddle-faddle. To be sure, cargoes from Cincinnati won't bring such a high price, but I'm still an able-bodied breadwinner. Besides, my trips will be shorter. I'll have more time to spend with you, and maybe I can get a few days' work between trips."

"But it won't be the same as having you with us all the time, George."

"No, it won't, Father," Steve said. "I'm going to work too. I can do a man's work now. If everybody contributes, it won't take us long to save up enough to buy the land."

"You'll go to school and get as much education as you can, young man," said Father.

Steve grinned. "My schooling can wait till you come back to us for keeps."

Father looked from one face to another. "What is this? A rebellion?"

"Yes, sir," said Steve.

Father scowled. "I won't have it," he said angrily. "I can't argue with women, but if I have to, Steve, I'll give you a sound thrashing to knock some sense into that obstinate red head of yours."

Steve stood up to him without blinking. "All right, Father. But I warn you, it won't stop me from going to work."

Father stared at him for a moment, then burst out laughing. Steve flushed through his freckles.

"I'm not laughing at you, Stevie," Father said. "I'm laughing because if I don't I'll give way and cry like a woman."

He rushed out of the kitchen, and they heard him puttering around in the store. The young people slowly resumed their packing, while Mother began to prepare dinner.

A few minutes later, Father reappeared in the kitchen doorway, blowing his nose.

"Here, here," he said brusquely. "We don't have to move out of the storeboat till Saturday. Miss Biddy, can't you hurry up dinner so these young folks can go ashore and see the city?"

"It will be ready directly," said Mother, replenishing the fire from the dwindling pile of wood beside the stove. "Meantime, suppose you boys wash up and put on shoes and stockings. We're in the city now."

After dinner Steve excused himself and dashed off the

boat, leaving the others deep in discussion of the problem of keeping livestock without a farm. He raced along the water-front, dodging in and out between horses and wagons and piles of merchandise, until he came to the "General Pike." He hitched up his pantaloons and walked up to the gangplank.

A lean bronzed watchman sat on an upturned box on the deck, smoking a clay pipe and whittling at a piece of pine. "Howdy," said Steve. "When does the 'General Pike' sail?"

The watchman took his pipe out of his mouth. "She ain't ready to go nowheres yet," he said. "She's waiting for a new valve to come down from Pittsburgh."

"Is General Harrison aboard?"

"Him? No, he's in North Bend, where he lives."

"Oh. Well, is his son Mr. William Harrison about?"

The watchman lighted his pipe again. "Him? Well, you might find him in his law office on Front Street, or again you might find him in the Cincinnati Hotel. What do you want with him?"

"I know his father, the general," Steve said, "and I thought he might let me see the engine."

"Well," said the watchman, removing his pipe to spit at a dragonfly that poised on the railing, "I might let you do that, if you won't touch nothing."

Steve thanked him and marched up the gangplank. He wandered through the boat, looking at the big open side-wheels, the bunkroom for the crew, the cabins for passengers, the messroom and pantry, and finally the single engine with its upright and stationary cylinders down in the hold. He climbed up into the pilot's house and looked out.

When he went back on deck, the watchman was still whittling. "Ever see a steamboat before, son?" he asked.

"Oh, yes. I come from Pittsburgh. I've seen the 'Enterprise,' the 'Despatch,' the 'Aetna,' the 'Buffalo,' the 'New Orleans,' the 'Constitution'—"

The watchman waved him down. "You don't have to read me no wharf register, young man. What do you think of the 'General Pike'?"

Steve hesitated. "Well," he said finally, "I prefer a high-pressure engine, with the boilers on deck instead of below. I think it's more practical for river travel."

The man laughed. "Think you know a lot, don't you, son?"

"Yes, I do. I know the 'Washington' is the best river boat ever built."

The watchman snorted. "The 'Washington'! Built by a man that don't know the meaning of the law. Thinks he can run steamboats without a Fulton and Livingston license."

Steve clenched his fists. "Would you mind stepping on shore?" he said hotly. "I'd like to pitch into you."

The man took his pipe out of his mouth again and gaped. Then he began to smile.

"Regular banty rooster, ain't you, son?" he said amiably. "Well, it's too hot for a fight, and I wouldn't be surprised if you'd lick me. If Captain Shreve's a friend of yours, I won't say no more."

"You'd better not," said Steve.

His face still burned as he strode down the gangplank and then slackened his pace. He began to count the boats moored along the waterfront. When he reached the seventh Kentucky boat loaded with coal, iron or dry goods, a man hailed him.

"Ain't you from Pittsburgh, son? Seems to me I used to see you down by the river."

"Hello, Mr. Ames!" Steve cried. "We've come here to live."

They had a long talk, and then Steve shook hands and moved on. He added to his count four keelboats, the schooner "Maria" bound for Boston by way of New Orleans with a cargo of flour and lard, the barge "Peacock" about to set sail for Maysville, four large scows carrying timber, building stones for New Orleans, and salt from the Kanawha works. And there were six flatboats swarming with emigrants and their livestock.

He stood a while on the bank to watch the horse-drawn ferryboat come in from Covington and Newport across the river. Three militiamen in blue uniforms and cocked hats piled off the ferry as it struck the shore.

The big Cincinnati Hotel opposite the landing place caught his eye, and he strolled over to see if he could spot the general's son. Men came and went through the open door, and the veranda was lined with loungers in shirt-sleeves with their chairs tilted against the wall.

As he passed, he heard disconnected snatches of conversation that aroused his interest.

"There'll be two bands in the parade tomorrow. . . ."

"I tell you, there won't be much emigration into slave states, because there's no work for white men. . . ."

"But the Erie canal will be only the beginning of a network of inland waterways. . . ."

"Shreve showed them, didn't he?"

Steve grinned at the last speaker and received a friendly wave of the hand in reply. Embarrassed at being caught eavesdropping, he began to run and did not stop until he came to the big stores on the crowded Main Street. Here he caught up with David and Susan.

"Oh, Steve," Susan breathed, "have you ever in all your life seen so many elegantly dressed ladies?"

"I see some that ain't so well decked out," said Steve, nodding toward a backwoods woman in a coarse brown dress of knee length.

"Susan and I've seen girls and even grown ladies without shoes," said David excitedly.

"Well, I wish Mother hadn't made me wear them," Steve grumbled. "Look at those boys. They ain't wearing shoes."

"But you look better," said Susan primly.

"I guess I don't care much about looking dressed up," said Steve. "Did Father decide what to do with Bessie and the geese and chickens?"

"Oh, yes," Susan replied. "Mr. Riddle came down to the boat, and he says he has room for them in his backyard. What's more, we can store our furniture and goods in his warehouse until we need them. My, isn't it hot?"

"And we're going to stay at Mr. Rice's boardinghouse across the street from the United States bank," said David, skipping to keep up with the other two.

"Well," said Steve, as he almost collided with a portly gentleman in a tall black beaver hat, "I can't give you any news, except that I saw the 'General Pike' and she's nothing elegant, and there's going to be a parade tomorrow."

"We know all about the parade," said Susan loftily. "There'll be a barbecue and games and contests too. Mr.

Riddle says you're not to wear your best bib and tucker if you expect to enjoy yourself."

David began to complain. "My feet hurt. These old shoes are too little. Let's go home."

As they approached the waterfront on the way back, they were just in time to see a small two-masted schooner skim into the harbor. Steve broke into a run and reached the landing ahead of the crowd.

At the bows of the neatly painted little vessel stood a white man and four well-dressed men with dark skins and high cheekbones, two dark women in American clothes, and a boy.

"Indians!" The word ran through the crowd.

A handsome elderly man pushed past Steve and approached the water's edge, unmindful of the mud.

"Welcome to Cincinnati!" he said in a deep clear voice.

"That's Judge Burnet," someone whispered.

"Good day, friend," called the tallest of the Indians. "Will you and several of the good citizens of Cincinnati come on board?"

Judge Burnet bowed, and turning to look through the crowd behind him, he chose five men, calling them by name. Then he noticed Steve.

"You too, boy. You and the Indian lad may find something to talk about."

Steve's face shone. He climbed into a skiff with the men, and they were helped on board the schooner.

Judge Burnet shook hands with all the Indians and Captain Dean, the white man. The others followed suit.

The tall Indian explained that they had left Rome, New York, on the first of June to enter new lands and claim them on behalf of the Iroquois Confederacy, and were now on the way home.

"You've made the trip very quickly," said the judge. "I presume the schooner was waiting for you down river."

"We made the entire trip with the schooner," said the Indian with a smile.

"How is that possible?"

"We came by way of Wood Creek, Oneida Lake, the Oswego river, and Lake Ontario. Then we had the schooner carted on wheels eleven miles around Niagara Falls, set sail again on Lake Erie, entered the Glaise river, and had another portage of eight and a half miles to the Miami river. We followed the Miami to its junction with the Ohio, and here we are."

"Remarkable!" exclaimed the judge.

"We'll show you our speed," said the Iroquois, and he made a signal to the crew. They manned the ropes, and in a moment the boat sailed out of the harbor and up the river with flapping sails and creaking masts.

"She fairly flies," the judge agreed. "Do you intend to return to Rome without disembarking from the schooner?"

"By all means. We'll follow the Ohio to Pittsburgh, then the Allegheny to the point nearest the headwaters of the Genesee. That will be our last portage."

While listening closely, Steve and the Iroquois boy had been eyeing each other steadily. When they began to talk, both of them asked many questions, and Steve soon found himself trying to explain the "General Pike" to the Indian.

"Ain't there any steamboats at all on the Great Lakes?" he asked.

The other boy shook his head. "No, and I never heard of them until today."

The schooner tacked about and skimmed back down the river near the Kentucky shore. As they approached Newport, the tall Iroquois fired his gun into the air and gave a toast: "The patriotism and bravery of Kentucky!"

The ship tacked again and glided across the river into the harbor of Cincinnati. He fired once more and gave another toast: "Free trade and no slavery!"

Everybody on board cheered. The cry was taken up by the crowd on shore until the sound re-echoed.

Then with more handshaking, the Americans said good-by and climbed down into the waiting skiff. The little schooner glided out into the channel and sailed away at a great rate, her sails puffed out with wind.

Steve paused long enough to thank Judge Burnet for inviting him aboard, then dodged through the crowd and raced to the storeboat. The rest of the family were standing on the roof in the blazing sunlight, watching the schooner disappear up the river. He leaped on board and hoisted himself up beside them, hot and breathless with excitement.

"What happened to you?" Susan asked. "We couldn't find you anywhere in the crowd."

"Of course you couldn't," Steve panted. "I was taking a little ride up the river with the Indians."

Chapter XXIII

SURPRISE

FATHER was so incredulous of Steve's account that he went below to get out his map and trace for himself the voyage of the Indian schooner.

In a few minutes he came to the foot of the ladder and shouted up to the roof. "Come here, folks! I want to show you on the map. The boy's right!"

It was stuffy in the kitchen as they all bent over the map unfolded on the table.

"See! See!" cried Father, disregarding the perspiration that rolled down his face. "By jingoes, those were smart Indians!"

Brownie and Patch lay stretched out under the table, panting with the heat. Father stepped on Brownie's tail, but she did not yelp. She only looked up at him reproachfully and shifted her position.

Suddenly Patch lifted her head and cocked her ears forward. Steve straightened up. "I thought I heard an Indian war whoop," he said.

"So did I," Susan said. She stepped to the window and cupped one hand behind her ear.

Everybody listened. The sound was repeated, each time a little nearer. Then they heard the strains of a fiddle. They looked at one another.

"If that's not Katy, I'll go bite an alligator," Steve said finally.

He gave a whoop and collided with Father in a rush for the hallway. They reached the roof just in time to see Pappy, in tatters and thinner than ever, climbing on deck from a strange raft made of logs and driftwood.

"Hello, the boat!" Pappy cackled, brandishing Katy and a bundle tied up in a red bandanna. "Hello, the ornery, low-down imitation of a storeboat!"

"Pappy, you old fool!" roared Father. "Steve, help him with his plunder. The old scoundrel!"

Pappy waved the boy aside and mounted the ladder to the roof. Mother, Susan and David scrambled up the hatchway, and there was such dancing and leaping that David fell off into the muddy water between the storeboat and the next barge. But he laughed harder than anybody when he clambered back on board, and no one thought to tell him to change into dry clothes.

"Come, Pappy," said Mother, "let me fix you some bacon and eggs. You must be hungry, and supper won't be ready for a long time."

"That'll taste mighty good after the scant vittles I've had," said Pappy, smacking his lips.

Down below, while the bacon and eggs sizzled in the frying pan, and the dogs pushed against his legs and stood up to lick his face, Pappy played tune after tune before he could trust himself to speak. Finally he stopped and squinted up at Father.

"Why in the name of little green parakeets and lightning bugs did you have to go off and leave me?" he demanded.

"I couldn't find you," Father protested. He paused and reddened.

"Did you miss some money, George?" asked Pappy.

"Well, yes."

"Davie, fetch me my plunder. It's over yonder on the floor."

David handed him the bundle tied up in the red bandanna.

"It's mighty heavy," he said.

Pappy chuckled as he untied the corners of the handkerchief and spread it out on the table. Gold and silver coins clinked and several rolled off on the floor. The Doaks gasped.

"Is that storeboat money?" Father asked.

"'Tain't all of it, George. I didn't catch him quick enough."

"Didn't catch whom?"

"Wilkins," said Pappy in surprise.

Mother set a plate before him, and he began to eat like a man half starved.

"Do you mean Wilkins stole our money?" asked Father.

"I thought you knew that, George," said Pappy, with his mouth full.

"How was I to know?" said Father. "I don't care to tell you what I thought when you and the money disappeared at the same time."

Pappy cackled. "I reckon it did look like a hocus-pocus," he said, licking his knife. "But if I missed anything when Wilkins was around, I'd know who took it."

"But if you knew Wilkins had the money, why didn't you tell me and call the sheriff?"

"Because I didn't know anything about the money till

after the fight, and then I was halfway across the state of Kentuck."

"What fight?" asked Father.

"George," said Pappy, shaking his head, "for a man of parts, you do sometimes act more like a dizzard than any river man I ever knew. I'm talking about Wilkins."

"Why don't you begin at the beginning and tell us the whole story, Pappy?" Mother put in. "I'm a little confused myself."

Pappy pushed aside the empty plate and leaned back in his chair.

"Well," he drawled, "this is what happened. You recollect I set off to find Wilkins. Everywheres I went, Wilkins had been and gone because he hadn't no money, and bartenders knowed him too well to take his promises. But I knowed Wilkins would keep on trying. So I played a few billiards to pass the time."

Pappy stopped to scrape several bars on Katy.

"Go on, Pappy," Steve urged.

"Well, late in the evening I come back to a tavern and missed him again, but I heard he'd bought a critter with real money. I didn't stop to figure out where he got the money. I just took the nearest critter tied to a hitching-post, and set out with Katy under my arm."

"How did you know which way to go, Pappy?" asked Father.

"Bartender told me Wilkins's wife lives on the Lexington road, other side of Paris. Don't interrupt me, George. So I took out lickety-split after Wilkins. Didn't even wait for the ferry across the Licking river. Passed through Blue Licks like a streak of chain lightning on the way home.

After I'd went maybe twenty miles, maybe forty, I seed Mr. Wilkins a-lying under a tree with his head on a bundle, a-snoring like thunder. I tied my critter and laid Katy behind a bush. Then I tapped Mr. Wilkins on the face with a hunk of wood to wake him up."

Pappy paused and smiled contentedly. " 'Twas a pretty chunk of a fight while it lasted. Upshot was I butted him clean into the next county. When I come to, he was still a-sleeping peaceful with his head in a bramble patch. I brought his bundle along because I knowed he didn't come by it honest, and them gold eagles and silver money looked like old friends to me. I figured I'd better ax you about them, George."

Father drew a deep breath. "Pappy, you don't know how much this means to us."

Steve grinned. "I guess I'll have to go to school after all, won't I, Father?"

Father tweaked his freckled nose. "Do you realize, Pappy, you've saved our whole future?"

"That's all right, George. But when I got back to Maysville with that critter I'd borrowed, and found you'd gone off without me, I was mad enough to whip wildcats. For three days I was so wore out I couldn't even jangle my bones, but if I'd met up with you, I'd have beat your ears down flat."

"Well, I hope you won't try it," said Father, slapping him on the back. "Do you know we're rich now? Mr. Riddle's paid off, and all the money belongs to us. That includes you too, Pappy."

"Me, George? What use have I got for money?"

"You earned it."

"Nothing of the sort," said the old man indignantly. "That was my own private, personal fight. I won't have none of your money."

Mother beckoned to Father and drew him off into the bedroom, where their voices were muffled by the thin partition.

"Did you see the schooner going up river, Pappy?" asked Steve.

"Did I see it? Passed right by it!"

"Steve went on board with the Indians," David said, wriggling in his chair.

"Was them Indians?" said Pappy. "Thought they was West Indians. Where'd they come from?"

Steve pushed the map toward Pappy and traced the course of the schooner again.

"Well, don't that beat the Dutch!" Pappy exclaimed admiringly. "First thing you know, folks'll be traveling all over the country in boats. Ask a man to go bear hunting in the cane-brakes, and he'll say, 'Wait a moment till I get my schooner.'"

"Let's put sails on the storeboat and see how fast she'll go!" David proposed. "Then we can hunt bears."

"'Taint practical," said Pappy. "She steers slow. Stevie, how did you and your paw make out without me?"

"Oh, we got on," Steve answered. "But we hankered after you and Katy."

David broke in excitedly. "When the floods came, Susie and me had to shove logs and things away from the boat with poles."

"Do pray tell," said Pappy. "I didn't have no crew on my raft, so I got stove in once or twice."

"Father says this is the worst flood he ever saw," said Steve.

"Oh, your father's too young to remember the flood of 1789. That was a real flood. Every ninnyhammer that built his cabin too near the banks found hisself a-traveling down the river whether he wanted to or not. Why, half the early settlers in the West got their start that way."

Mother and Father appeared in the doorway.

"Now, now, Pappy," warned Father. "Stick to the truth."

"I thought you was in the other room, George," Pappy drawled. "Well, anyway, I'm satisfied them two cabins I did see floating down river with all hands aboard never went back up river again."

"It must have been a bad flood," Susan remarked, her brown eyes twinkling.

"'Twas," said Pappy. "It's the absolute truth I never went ashore once till the 1789 flood was over. When I got hungry, all I had to do was reach out and grab a chicken off a log as she passed. That is, I didn't go ashore but once."

"What happened that time?" asked Susan.

"Well, that was an accident that might happen to any man, even in low water. I was a-napping one hot day, and when I woke up I was pretty near drownded. My craft was two feet under water. Well, I jumped overboard and towed her to shore, and what do you think I found?" He paused dramatically.

"Go on," said David breathlessly.

"Well, I found a yellow-bellied catfish had flipped his

tail clean through the bottom of my boat. The waters was pouring in so fast he was stuck there."

When the laughter had subsided, Mother crossed the room and laid her hand on the old man's shoulder.

"Pappy," she said, "there's one pair of shoes left in the store, and we think they'd fit you. Then George is going to take you to Mr. Riddle's dry goods store and help you buy some new clothes and a gold watch."

Pappy's face went blank. "Why, what's the matter with what I got on?"

Mother smiled. "They're all right, Pappy, except that they need considerable darning, and I think you ought to have something to wear while I work on them."

"Don't that beat all!" Pappy said. "I throw away my duds when they fall off, but I never thought of sewing them back on. And I never thought I'd see the day when somebody'd offer me a gold watch. Are you crazy, George?"

"Pretty near," said Father jovially. "Let's buy everything that's left in the store! The shoes are yours, Pappy. Davie, you can have the Barlow knife. Steve, how'd you like the compass? And, Susie, you'd better try on your bonnet."

The young people shrieked and raced into the store to get their share.

"I don't know what to do about the rest of the things," said Father. "I could take the scythe. Is there anything you want, Miss Biddy?"

"Yes, George. I'd like to have the yellow calico. I don't know exactly what to do with it, unless we could put a dry goods flag on our new house. But I want it anyway, to remind me of the storeboat."

Chapter XXIV

THE FOURTH OF JULY

THE Fourth dawned clear and bright with a golden sunrise. It was hot even at that early hour. The boys bounded out of bed and put on clean pink calico shirts and pantaloons of blue jean, such as they wore every day. But Susan dressed up in her best long flowered dimity dress and black slippers, and tied a blue silk sash about her slender waist.

When they went into the kitchen to wash, they found Mother preparing breakfast in a white lawn dress, protected by a huge blue gingham apron. Father was shaving before the mirror in his white duck pantaloons.

Pappy, shining with cleanliness and elegant in new blue and white striped duck pantaloons and a coat of dark blue jean, was pacing up and down uneasily. Occasionally he stopped to wiggle his toes inside the new black shoes.

"Ain't no more water aboard the boat," he announced. "Took all there was to get me cleaned up. Ain't I a popinjay?"

"You look very handsome, Pappy," said Susan. "But you ought to have a ruffled shirt and a high neckcloth."

Pappy looked sheepish. "Nobody's going to get me into them furbelows."

"Oh, yes, I am," said Mother serenely.

"But, Pappy," Steve protested, "if you wear your new clothes you can't enter the contests. You'll spoil them."

"I ain't fixing to enter no contests," said Pappy. "Me and Katy'll find ourselves some other amusement."

"You boys had better fetch some water from the hotel," said Mother, breaking an egg into the frying pan.

When the boys came back with two pailfuls of water, breakfast was on the table. Pappy was wearing his ruffled shirt and a guilty look, but no neckcloth. Father was perspiring in a white frilled shirt with a low stock and his tailed blue broadcloth coat.

Already they could hear drums and fifes. People thronged up and down the waterfront, and new skiffs were arriving filled with families from neighboring settlements.

Mother insisted upon washing the dishes and making the beds, but it was still early when they locked the dogs inside and went ashore.

The streets were swarming. Fine ladies in muslin and white embroidered lawn with little parasols rubbed elbows with barefoot women and children from the back country dressed in faded calico. There were plain farmers in blue jeans and straw hats, and men in fine broadcloth, in thin white cotton jackets without neckcloths or waistcoats, and in rough homespun. Boys of every age and description shouted, whistled, and dodged in and out among the crowds.

Every half hour cannon were fired. Military bands in red uniforms with gold braid paraded up and down the streets. Now and then a horse, frightened by the noise, reared up on its hind legs and attempted to bolt through the horde of pedestrians who were jostled off the sidewalks. Soldiers in brilliant uniforms began to assemble near the landing, and at eleven o'clock the parade began with a blare of trumpets. One of the bands strutted at the head of the procession. Then followed three companies of volunteers, first the rifle corps and then two companies of infantry, marching in fours. The other band brought up the rear. As they swung past, everybody in the streets fell in behind them, two by two.

Pappy, limping along in his new shoes beside Susan, drawled in a high voice, "Looks like a mighty funny parade to me. Nobody to see it, because all the folks in six counties is in it."

While the first band played "Hail Columbia," and the second burst out with "Yankee Doodle," the procession marched up the street and up the hill to the big brick Presbyterian church. Most of the well-dressed ladies took the front pews, and the rest crowded into the church until there was no more standing room. The Doaks found benches at one side.

The Fourth of July ceremony began with a prayer and a psalm read by the minister. Next Judge Burnet rose and read the Declaration of Independence in his clear ringing voice. After that the congregation joined in solemn singing:

> Fathers, sires, heroes brave,
> Who fought and died for liberty,
> The heavenly boon we swear to save,
> Whilst Freedom has a votary.

The heat was so oppressive that the ladies in the congregation brought out their fans, and the men mopped their faces with their handkerchiefs.

After the national hymn and the amen, the orator of the day stepped up to the pulpit to make his address. It was General William Henry Harrison, resplendent in his gold-trimmed uniform.

The familiar booming voice resounded in the church. His listeners held their heads higher as he spoke of the spirit of liberty which made it possible for men of all nations to live in freedom, comfort and plenty, united as a band of brothers under a common flag. He closed with a plea that the gates of America might be forever kept open for the oppressed of the Old World.

There was complete silence as he sat down. Here and there an old man in the faded uniform of a Revolutionary soldier wiped his eyes and bowed his head.

In conclusion another patriotic hymn was sung softly:

> When first the sun o'er ocean glowed,
> And earth unveiled her virgin breast,
> Supreme 'mid nature's vast abode,
> Was heard the Almighty's dread behest.
> Rise, Columbia, brave and free,
> Poise the earth, and rule the sea.

Afterward the crowds swarmed out into the hot sunlight and trooped past the old burying-ground to the open field and the cottonwood grove behind the Courthouse.

Here crude tables of rough deal had been set up on saw-horses, and busy housewives were laying out platters of bar-becued beef, pork and venison which had been roasted in Indian style over an open pit. There were piles of good sliced bread and fresh butter, large baskets of fruit, nuts and raisins, as well as cakes and pies of all sorts.

"It takes a powerful chance of truck to feed such a heap of folks," said Pappy, smacking his lips.

Some took the food in their hands and wandered off to the shade of a little wood near by, but others sat down on the grass where they were, or stood about in groups, eating and chattering. The vivid uniforms of the militia stood out among the light dresses of the ladies.

Pappy and the Doaks spread one of Father's clean handkerchiefs on the grass and heaped it with bread and meat, then sat down in a circle around it.

Suddenly the general's voice boomed out at them.

"Good morning, Doak! Glad to see you arrived safely with your little flock. This is my son, William Henry Harrison, Junior." He indicated a tired-looking young man beside him.

The young man bowed. Father rose to shake hands.

The general beamed at the group. "I look forward to another conversation with you all. Doak and I may settle the problems of our great country over a friendly bowl one day soon."

His eyes wandered, and he smiled and bowed to other groups.

"Well," he said, with a little nod, "I see many of my old friends in this patriotic gathering. I shall have to bestir myself if I want to speak to half of them. Good day, friends."

"Good day, General. Good day, Mr. Harrison."

The two men strolled away.

Steve paused in the middle of a mouthful. "There comes Judge Burnet," he said.

The others looked up.

"And see who's with him!" Steve scrambled to his feet. "Simon!"

At the sound of his name, Simon's face lighted up and he cleared the space between them in three strides.

"I've been looking for you," he said, dropping to the grass beside Susan.

"Why, Simon, I wouldn't have known you! You look so—" Susan stopped and colored.

"So dressed up? But you see I'm in the city now." He looked down at his frilled shirtfront and buff pantaloons. "I'm not used to them yet, though."

Suddenly his face reddened. "I—I'm sorry, I forgot to speak to your mother and father and Pappy and the boys."

"We noticed you were here," said Pappy drily.

Simon grinned and tried to greet them formally, but everybody laughed.

Judge Burnet came up and stood over them. "I see you've found your friends, Simon. You look as smiling as a basket of chips. Why, hello! here's my young red-headed friend of the Indian schooner!"

Steve grinned. Simon jumped to his feet and made the introductions.

"Won't you join us, Judge?" said Father.

Judge Burnet sat down beside him. "I can stay but a moment. I seem to have mislaid my wife in the crowd. Mr. Doak, Simon tells me you brought Riddle's new store-boat down river for him."

The judge wrapped a piece of barbecued pork in a slice of bread and stuffed it into his mouth.

"Yes," said Father. "It was a lucky chance for us. I've been wanting to move to Cincinnati for some years."

"Not making a mistake, Doak," the judge said, taking out his handkerchief to wipe his fingers. "Come around and see me within the next few days. I want to talk to you. And now I've got to go and find Mrs. Burnet."

He grunted as he got to his feet, and said his good-bys.

"I'll be home later, Judge," said Simon, reaching for another piece of venison. "He's letting me stay at his home till I get settled," he added as the judge departed.

"I thought you weren't coming till fall, Simon," Susan said.

"So did I," he answered between mouthfuls. "But Judge Burnet wrote me a letter saying he needed a clerk right away, and he'd pay me wages while I studied if I'd come."

"Did you drive your horses all the way, Simon?" asked David.

"No, it was too far. I took passage on the packet."

"How many want a piece of cake?" asked Steve. "I'm still hungry."

"Fetch enough cake for us all, Steve," Mother suggested.

When he returned with the cake he reported that one of the tables was being removed.

"We'd better hurry if we want anything to eat," he said.

In a few minutes Pappy raised his head to listen. "I hear a fiddle."

"They're getting ready to dance over yonder," said Simon, pointing to a far corner of the field.

"Oh, that's where they took the table," Steve said. "The fiddler's sitting on it."

Pappy wiped his mouth with the back of his hand and picked up Katy. "Well, I reckon I've had about enough vittles, and Katy's a-raring to go."

Simon turned to Susan. "Do you like square dances?"

She nodded. "Let's go with Pappy."

They sauntered across the grassy field, and soon Pappy had his new shoes off and was seated on the table beside the whiskered old fiddler, tuning up Katy before beginning a new set.

Simon and Susan took their places in one of the two rows of rosy-cheeked girls and boys facing each other, partners side by side. The caller leaned over the edge of the table to spit through his whiskers, and drew his bow across the strings.

"Honor your partners, one and all," he sounded off as he and Pappy began to play.

Clapping, dancing, laughing at the fiddler's calls, they skipped through the figures as he sang them out.

First lady out to the gent on the right,
Cheat or swing or do as you like;
Swing him if you love him and cheat him if you don't.
First lady lead to the right;
Swing that gent that looks so neat,
And then the fellow with the great big feet;
And then the one with the freckled nose,
And then the man with the store-bought clothes.
Swing them all eight.
Allemande left with your left hand pard;
Grand change right and wrong
As you come around.
Right foot, left foot, hay foot, straw foot,
Meet your pard and take a back track,
Meet your pard and promenade eight.
Swing that Injun, swing that squaw,
Swing that fellow from O-hi-O.

But when Simon and Susan met in the last figure and linked arms to swing, they did not stop with a single whirl. They smiled at each other and kept on swinging around and around on the grass.

"Wake up, Simon," Pappy drawled above the music.

They dropped their arms, and both flushed. They found the other six young people already lined up to begin the next set. Several girls tittered.

Susan backed out of the row of dancers, edged through the crowd who were watching, and started to walk away. Simon caught up with her and bent over her.

"I'm mighty sorry," he said. "Seems like when I got hold of your arm I couldn't let go."

She looked up at his pleasant tanned face, the brown hair brushed smoothly back, the damp curls at the nape of his neck.

"I—I felt silly," she said.

"I feel silly every time I see you," he said. "Tongue-tied."

She glanced up at him through her eyelashes. "Why, Simon Winthrop!" she said. "You told me in Steubenville that there were lots of things you wanted to say, and you'd say them when you got to Cincinnati. Here we are, and now you tell me you're tongue-tied!"

He reddened. "Well, I wanted to—to ask you if I might call on you."

"I'll wager that wasn't what you meant to say at all," Susan said mischievously.

He shook his head. "It wasn't. But I'm not going to say more until I have a house fit for you to live in and money to buy you silk dresses and India shawls. Now—are you still mad at me?"

She laughed softly. "No, Simon. But I can't answer your question till you ask it."

"It may be years," he said.

"I can wait, Simon."

"You can? Well, promise me one thing. If any other man asks you to marry him, will you tell me and let me lick him?"

"I promise."

Simon seized her hand and began to run with her. "Come on! I've got to run or wrestle or something, or I'll let out a roar like a ring-tailed screamer!"

Laughing and panting, she tried to keep up with him. Finally, brushing the curls out of her eyes, she slowed down.

"You'd do better in the contests than trying to run a race with me," she said.

"Come on!" he shouted. "I'll show them!"

They edged into a group of people lined up to watch a race.

The starter called out, "Any more? Who else wants to enter this race? The prize is this here elegant layer cake, one foot across and six inches high, by actual count. The starting point is this here line. The runners will circle yonder oak and come back to the starting point."

Simon stepped out. "I'll take your cake, sir."

The other contestants roared. One of them, a well-built, sunburned man with deep blue eyes and bristling eyebrows, smiled and said, "That's my cake, young man." Then he threw back his head and gave a long toot like a boat horn.

Simon laughed and they shook hands. The runners toed

the line, the starter gave the signal by firing a pistol into the air, and they were off.

Down the field they tore, skidded around the tree, and raced back. The crowd yelled and leaped in their excitement, and parted to let the runners through. Simon and the man with the eyebrows crossed the line at exactly the same moment.

"Two winners!" bellowed the starter. "Has anybody a sword to cut the cake in half?"

The other winner mopped his face with a blue bandanna and turned to Simon. "The prize is yours, young man," he said. "I don't care much for cake."

With some protest, Simon accepted the prize and presented it to Susan.

"I'm mighty proud," she said. "But I guess you'll have to carry it, because it's so big."

They wandered over to another large group. Here wrestling matches were in progress. Just as they got there, they saw Steve, dirty and perspiring, give a mighty heave, overturn a stocky boy, and pin his arms to his sides by sitting on him.

A voice beside Susan remarked, "There's a good boy."

Susan looked up into the deep-set eyes of the man who had raced with Simon. "That's my brother," she said.

"You should be proud of him." The man smiled and walked away.

David came elbowing through the crowd. "I won a race for younger boys," he said. "I got three apples, but I ate them. They were sort of wrinkled anyway. Did you see Steve? That's the third time he's won."

Steve had got up and brushed off the dust. He came over, grinning. "Where'd you get the cake?" he asked.

Susan replied, "Simon won it in a race."

"Did you, Simon? Good for you." Steve lowered his voice and said, "Have you seen a man around here, mighty sunburned, with bushy eyebrows and deep blue eyes?"

"That sounds like the man who finished the race with Simon," Susan said. "He was right here a minute ago."

Steve and David looked at Simon with something like awe in their eyes.

"Do you mean you can run as fast as he can?" asked Steve.

"Yes, he can," Susan declared.

The boys whistled. "I'll tell you something," Steve confided. "That man gets all the prizes and then gives them away. Dave and I think he must be Mike Fink, because he can outrun, outjump, and outwrestle anything on two legs, less'n it might be you, Simon."

"Mike Fink!" Susan gasped. "Why, he did make a noise like a boat horn, didn't he, Simon? Let's find him and look at him again. He's brown but he doesn't act like a boatman."

"They're always polite in front of ladies," said Steve. "But it's Mike Fink, all right."

"Who is Mike Fink?" Simon asked.

When they told him, he too whistled. The four of them set out to look for the man with the eyebrows. They searched among the wrestlers, the runners, the jumpers, the target shooters. He was nowhere to be found.

Finally Susan said, "I'm getting tired. I'd like to find

Mother and Father and sit down a while. Besides, Simon can't carry that big cake around forever."

"I'm tired, too," Steve admitted. "I've had enough wrestling for such a hot day."

At last they spied Mother and Father sitting under a cottonwood tree. The very man they were seeking lay on the grass beside them, leaning on one elbow as he talked earnestly to Father.

"It is Mike Fink," said Steve positively. "Father said he knew him."

They approached timidly. The man looked up and stopped talking.

"Here's my family," said Father, "and Simon Winthrop, a young man who has come to read law in Judge Burnet's office. Young folks, here's a man you've been talking about for some time."

Steve stepped up and held out his hand. "I'm mighty glad to make your acquaintance, Mr. Fink."

"Well, well, if it isn't the young wrestler! Why call me Mr. Fink?"

Steve reddened. "I thought—"

"Ain't you Mr. Fink?" David blurted out.

The man threw back his head and laughed. "No, whoever he is, I'm not Mr. Fink."

Father slapped his thigh and roared. "Oho, Captain, that's a good joke! Haven't you ever heard of the fabulous keelboatman, Mike Fink?"

"Oh, that rascal. But whatever gave you the notion I was Mike Fink?"

Steve grinned. "Because you make a noise like a boat

horn and you can outrun, outjump and outfight any man in Cincinnati."

"I'm not so sure I'm such a champion as all that," said the man, with a glance at Simon and the big cake he carried. "This young man could teach me a great deal."

David planted himself before him. "If you're not Mike Fink, then who are you?"

"My name is Shreve."

"Captain Shreve!" the young Doaks chorused.

They began to fire questions at him.

"Did the 'Washington' make the Falls all right?"

"Did you bring the 'Washington' with you?"

"Did you win the law case?"

Finally Captain Shreve threw up his hands. "One question at a time, if you please."

"I told you my children were interested in you," said Father, laughing.

"Let's all sit down," said the captain. "Now! The 'Washington' steamed up the Falls as if they were riffles."

Father broke in. "And the city of Louisville gave a banquet to celebrate the first real and final proof that the Falls can be navigated by steam. Captain Shreve was the toast of the town."

"Any flat-bottomed boat could do it," said Shreve. "As for your other questions, the 'Washington' is in the harbor here at Cincinnati. I got here about noon. And you shall all have a little voyage tomorrow."

"Hurray! hurray!"

Steve began to turn cartwheels and David jumped up and down.

"Now as for the lawsuit against me," the captain resumed,

"I've won one decision, but Livingston is appealing to a higher court. I expect to be involved in suits for many years to come."

"But you'll win in the end, won't you, sir?" asked Steve, settling down at the captain's feet.

"I mean to," Shreve replied grimly.

They heard a yell, and Pappy swooped down upon them, coat tails flying, Katy and his shoes in his hands.

"Henry Shreve, you old steam-spouting alligator-horse!"

He and the captain thumped each other on the back and grinned.

"Where'd you get the clothes, Pappy? And why don't you wear your shoes?"

"George dressed me up like this," said Pappy. "But can't nobody make me wear them shoes again—excepting Miss Biddy here. Captain, would you admire to know what time of day it is? George even give me a little bitty clock that tells time by the minutes."

He pulled the enormous gold watch out of his pocket. "It's exactly—exactly—what's that little figure, Steve?"

"It's twenty minutes after four o'clock," said Steve, peering at the dial.

"Tarnation!" Shreve exclaimed. "I had no idea it was so late. I must find Judge Burnet. Doak, will you come with me? You may be interested in one of the things I want to talk over with him."

Father and the captain walked off together, and the others watched until they were lost in the crowd.

Then Steve jumped up. "Who wants to go down to the landing with me and take a look at the 'Washington'?" he asked.

"Let's all go back to the boat," Mother suggested. "I keep thinking how hot it must be for Brownie and Patch locked inside on a day like this."

Simon's face fell and he got to his feet slowly.

"Can't you join us, Simon?" Mother said. "We'll have a bite of supper after a while."

His face cleared as he bent over to pick up the cake. "I don't have to go anywhere this time," he said.

They strolled across the field, past the church and down the long hill to the waterfront.

"There's the 'Washington,' I guess," said Steve, pointing. His voice cracked with excitement.

"Yes, sir," said Pappy. "Ain't she a beauty? She's over twice as long as the storeboat and her top deck's twice as high."

"She looks like a dismasted frigate," Mother observed.

"Now, Miss Biddy," Pappy scolded, "don't you go poking your fun at the finest boat on the western waters."

"I want to go aboard," said David.

"No, not yet," Steve said, still staring eagerly at the steamboat. "Let's wait till tomorrow when Captain Shreve can tell us all about everything."

That night after supper, when dusk was settling over the city and the fireflies flickered in the darkening streets, the Doaks, Simon, and Pappy sat on the roof of the storeboat to watch the rockets flare up and lose themselves among the earliest stars above the Courthouse.

The cool breeze from the river touched their faces, and they could faintly hear the sounds of festivity in the taverns along the waterfront.

Father reached out and patted Mother's hand. "I know

I shouldn't speak up till tomorrow when I find out more," he said, "but I can't keep still a minute longer."

"What's gnawing at your vitals, George?" Pappy drawled.

"Well, Henry Shreve and I had a talk with Judge Burnet about a company forming here in Cincinnati to manufacture fire engines, mill machinery, brass and copper castings, and chiefly engines for steamboats. They expect to have several furnaces, a lot of smith's forges, and at least a hundred workmen."

"Will they hire me, Father?" Steve interrupted eagerly.

"Not till you finish your schooling, Red," said Father. "Meantime they're looking for a manager."

"Meaning you, George?" asked Mother.

"Meaning me, if it suits all the partners."

"But what about living in the country?" asked Mother. "How could we have the farm, if you work in the city?"

"We could, on one condition," Father replied. "That's something you and I have spoken about more than once, Miss Biddy."

Mother nodded. "Pappy," she said, "I think George wants to ask you something."

"Go ahead, George," said Pappy, "as long as you don't make me stick to the truth."

"I'd like the truth this time," said Father seriously. "Would you like to settle down, Pappy?"

Pappy scratched his white head. "Well, George, it depends."

"I'm going to the land office tomorrow," Father said. "Then we have to draw up plans for the house. In that house I'd like to build a room for you, Pappy, as big or as little as you want. If you were there to boss the hired men and take care of Miss Biddy, I'd never worry while I was at the factory."

Pappy picked up Katy and drew the bow across the strings. Then he laid down the fiddle and blew his nose. The young people began to smile. He wiped his eyes with the back of his hand, and grinned at Father by the light of an exploding rocket.

"You goggle-eyed, bandy-legged, high-flying, hot-brained, tin-tailed son of a stuffed snapping turkle!" he said, and his voice broke. "You ain't noticed me heading back up river, have you? You didn't think you was going to get rid of me, did you?"

He struck up a tune and began to sing:

> 'Tis you can reap and mow, love,
> And I can spin and sew,
> And we'll settle on the banks of
> The pleasant O-hi-O

He paused with his bow in the air. "Did you ever notice, George, how old folks is generally sitting around grumbling about the present state of affairs? Young folks seem to be enjoying it or making arrangements to change it for the better. Now me, I can't see no possible improvement on the present. I reckon this is about the best day in my whole flea-bitten life!"

"Yes, but tomorrow's going to be even better," said Father.

"Indeed it is," Steve agreed, and his eyes sought out the "Washington" looming up in the twilight.

"And the day after tomorrow too," said Simon shyly, with his eyes on Susan's face.

1540